A game of "truth or dare" leaves Tess feeling like she doesn't measure up. Will making the gymnastics team prove she can excel?

"TESS THOMAS, YOU'RE NEXT." STEFANI MOTIONED HER onto the beam. Tess mounted, her knees weaker than they had ever been. Her ankle was getting warm now, and the throbbing was more noticeable. She could feel it swelling up. Carefully she stepped and then dipped her foot below the beam level. *No mistakes yet. Concentrate. Don't look around you.* A piece of sweaty hair slipped out of the knot and slid down the side of her cheek as she concentrated. *Come on. Back to the end of the beam and then cartwheel.*

And then, in what seemed like slow motion, she sensed her ankle give way and her foot slip off the board, pulling her body right along with it.

Secret Sisters: (se'-krit sis'-terz) n. Two friends who choose each other to be everything a real sister should be: loyal and loving. They share with and help each other no matter what!

Secret ✻ Sisters

Double Dare

Sandra Byrd

WATERBROOK
PRESS
COLORADO SPRINGS

DOUBLE DARE

PUBLISHED BY WATERBROOK PRESS

5446 North Academy Boulevard, Suite 200

Colorado Springs, Colorado 80918

A division of Bantam Doubleday Dell Publishing Group, Inc.

Scriptures in the Secret Sisters series are quoted from the
International Children's Bible, New Century Version,
copyright © 1986, 1988 by Word Publishing,
Dallas, Texas 75039. Used by permission.

The characters and events in this book are fictional,
and any resemblance to actual persons or events
is coincidental.

ISBN 1-57856-019-5

Printed in the United States of America

1998—First Edition

10 9 8 7 6 5 4 3 2 1

For my children, Sam and Elizabeth

I praise God because he made you in an amazing and wonderful way.
What he has done is wonderful. I know this very well.
Psalm 139:14

one

Birthday Blues?

Friday Night, January 17

"This is definitely the worst birthday I've ever had." Tess slumped down in the backseat. Staring out the window instead of looking at her family, she watched the lush winter Arizona landscape rush by. The syrupy smell of ripe oranges perfumed the air, but she hardly noticed. "First, I'm cut from the school play. When I get home after that little rejection, I find out all of my friends have called my mother and canceled on my slumber party. What am I? A loser?"

Tyler, Tess's eight-year-old brother, piped up, "Pizza was good, don't you think, old girl?"

"I guess so, Inspector," Tess mumbled. Usually she played along with Tyler's British accent, but tonight she wasn't in the mood. Tyler wanted to be a Scotland Yard investigator when he grew up. Britain was a long way away from their Scottsdale, Arizona, home, but that didn't stop him from practicing his language skills.

"I mean, I cleaned my room and everything," Tess

complained. "Now nobody can sleep over? It's bad enough that Joann and Katie canceled, but Erin?"

Erin Janssen was Tess's best friend and Secret Sister. Since both girls had only brothers, they chose one another as sisters, doing everything that the best of sisters would do for each other. They shared clothes and private thoughts and cried both tears of joy and sadness together.

"I'm sure her mother had a good reason for taking her with her tonight," Tess's mother consoled.

"How about we go glow bowling?" her dad suggested.

"What's glow bowling?" Tess muttered, looking at her hands.

"The bowling alley has black lights on, and the pins all glow in the dark. And they have neon decorations up. It might be fun," Mrs. Thomas said.

"You mean the four of us? Just our family?" Tess asked. She liked her family, but really, on her twelfth birthday she wanted her friends, too.

"What are we, dog food?" Tyler asked. "Don't answer that," he continued, looking at his sister's raised eyebrows.

"I guess we can go." Tess sighed.

A few minutes later they arrived at Prickly Pear Alley. "Hey, isn't that Erin's mom walking in the parking lot? And that looks like Erin!" Tess saw the stifled smiles on her family's faces.

"You guys," Tess burst out with happy realization, "you planned all along that Erin would be here!"

"Well, we did say she had somewhere important to go," her mom said.

As soon as her dad stopped the car, Tess jumped out and ran to meet her friend.

Erin hugged her and said, "Happy birthday! I guess I can't say I'm older and wiser than you anymore." She laughed. "Let's go."

Arm in arm they marched into the darkened bowling alley, squinting their eyes to adjust to the near blackout. "What do we do now?" Tess turned to ask her mother, who nudged her in the direction of the snack bar.

Nothing could have prepared Tess for the shock she received next.

two

Spare Me

Friday Night, January 17

There, waiting in the corner, were the kids from her class. *All* of them.

Spinning on her heels toward her parents, she squealed, "Mom and Dad, you planned this? What's going on?" She didn't know whether to laugh, cry, or die.

"Surprise!" the class yelled. Twenty-five white T-shirts gleamed in the dark and jumped up and down. Glow-in-the-dark laces in their bowling shoes looked like fifty criss-crossed worms writhing on the floor. The farthest five lanes were marked off for "The Thomas Party."

"Here." Her dad tossed her an oversized white T-shirt. "Put this on. The white will glow. Let me help you find some bowling shoes. What size?"

"Ah, eight," Tess answered, her voice a little softer now.

"Eight!" someone whispered behind her. "She has big feet."

Tess ducked her head, ignoring the barb, and made her way through the fog-machine steam to greet the other members of her class. Soon she partnered with Erin, Joann, and Katie, and they moved to one of the lanes. The other kids formed teams of four or five, too, mostly hanging out with the same people they hung out with at school.

Tess still couldn't believe they had pulled this all together without her knowing. No one at school had even hinted.

Just as she was ready to start bowling, she peered through the blinking strobe light and noticed Heidi hanging in the back. "Is she on a team?" Tess whispered to Erin.

"I don't know. I thought she was with those guys." Erin jerked her thumb at the empty lane next to them. "But they disappeared into the girls' bathroom."

Tess bowled, keeping one eye on Heidi.

Joann bowled next. "Look, I knocked them all down on the second ball!" she shouted. Tess rolled her eyes toward heaven. Yet something else Joann was good at.

"It's called a spare," Joann continued excitedly.

"Okay, Joann, then 'spare' me," Katie teased her, and Joann laughed along. Easygoing Katie knew just what to say to bring Joann back to earth.

"Look," Joann whispered to the others on her team. The girls on the next lane finally came out of the bathroom. Bright blue eye shadow sugared each of their lids, and rough strokes of deep red blush shone from several feet away.

"I like it," Katie said, and Tess and Erin giggled.

Tess's gaze returned to Heidi, who was still alone. "Let's ask Heidi to bowl with us."

"Oh, Tess, it'll mess up our scoring. We've already started," Joann said.

"And she won't want to stay with our team," Erin added. "She never stays in one place."

Katie said, "I guess she could play with us. But, um, you know how she wanders off and doesn't pay attention."

Heidi had mild Down syndrome. But she was sweet and gentle and never said anything hurtful.

"Heidi, want to bowl with us?" Tess asked her anyway. Tess was the hostess, after all.

"Yeah. Thank you." Heidi brightened up and lugged her ball toward their lane.

"Thanks for inviting me," she said. Her almond-shaped eyes sparkled as she approached the girls, a big white sweatshirt covering her large frame. "I never go to birthday parties." A stab of sorrow struck Tess's heart.

In spite of the other girls' reluctance, a few minutes later they all cheered, "Yeah! Way to go!" when Heidi's first ball didn't wobble into the gutter. Instead, it hit the outside left three pins. Heidi, grinning with pleasure, wandered over a few lanes to tell the others.

"I told you she wouldn't stay put," Erin said.

"Smile!" Tess's mother aimed her camera at them, snapped a picture, then hurried off to take some more.

"Well, I'll go ahead and bowl," Katie said. "Who knows when she might be back."

"Here," Joann said. "I bought us glow-in-the-dark glasses." She put on a pair. The green neon contrasted sharply with her deep cocoa skin.

"Joann, you are positively crazy," Tess said, slipping on a pair, too.

"Smile!" Tess's mom said. Then she snapped another picture.

"Hey, all you at the Thomas party," the announcer said as he lowered the music. "It's time to do the chicken dance. Russell and"—he leaned over to get the other name— "Kenny here have agreed to lead you in the dance." Just then some crazy clucking country-western song burst out from the speakers. A yellow strobe light whirled from the ceiling, slashing light through the darkness.

"You're joking," Erin said under her breath. "They have no dignity." Her fair skin glowed pinkish purple from the black lights, and she elbowed Tess as Kenny and Russell lifted their fists into their armpits and began to squat and squawk in time to the music.

"Hey, Tess, your dad can really cackle," Kenny called. Tess almost melted into the alley in distress.

"Dad!" she called out. He didn't listen but squawked along. And her mother was no help. She tapped her foot to the music, tossing popcorn into her mouth every couple of seconds in time to the beat.

"She eats popcorn all day now. Pregnancy cravings," Tess whispered to Erin. Tess's mother was four months pregnant, and Tess figured all weird behavior could be attributed to that. Glancing at the alley next to theirs, Tess noticed the Maybelline crew refused to do the chicken. The boys in the class, however, almost all joined in.

Not soon enough the chicken music screeched to an end, and normal music flowed from the loudspeakers again. "Thank you, Lord," Tess said softly, as she exhaled, and they all went back to the lanes.

After everyone had a chance to bowl two full games, the class gathered in the snack area to eat cake and ice cream and to watch Tess open presents. The mother of one of the made-up girls came early and marched her daughter into the bathroom to scrape off her makeup. Tess caught her mother looking on with a smile.

Tess's dad strode over from the main desk and handed out some thin black markers. "Here," he said. "Before anyone leaves, be sure to sign your name on the back of Tess's T-shirt so she'll remember you all when she's rich and famous." Erin looked at Tess in sympathy. Fathers could be such a problem.

Erin signed first, as "Erin Janssen, your S. Sis.," then passed the pen around. Kenny, of course, drew a chicken and signed his name under it. When it was Heidi's turn, she drew a heart on Tess's shoulder and put her name in it.

"Thanks for bowling on our team," Tess said to Heidi. She really meant it. Heidi had more going for her than some others Tess knew.

"You're welcome." Heidi smiled with pleasure.

After scraping the frosting off her piece of cake, Tess took a bite. Mmm. Marble cake. Her favorite.

"You had better open the presents, honey." Her mother handed one to her. "The parents will be here soon."

One by one Tess opened the gifts, getting some cool posters, a couple of paperbacks, a scrunchie pack, and some super-sized boxes of Lemon Heads. She was especially pleased by the day-by-day calendar from Erin. Each day had something interesting that had happened in history on that day, or a verse from the Bible, or a quote. She read today's: "Mohammed Ali, boxing champion, was born on this day. What do you excel in? Does that make you a champion in life?" Tess smiled. Her Secret Sis had found a perfect gift.

"Here's mine," Joann said. Unwrapping the carefully taped paper, Tess uncovered the book *How to Really Succeed in School.* For a minute she wasn't sure if Joann was kidding, but after seeing the earnest look on her friend's face, she decided Joann wasn't.

"Thanks," Tess said, not sure what else to say. Obviously, Joann thought Tess needed help in school. One by one the kids left the party until only Erin, Joann, and Katie were left.

"Thanks for coming, you guys," Tess said. "This was such a surprise!" She turned toward her parents. "I can't believe you invited the whole class."

"We hadn't meant to invite everyone, just the girls," Tess's mother explained. "But when we invited Devon, thinking it was a girl, and he called back to say he would love to come, we didn't want to uninvite him. So we just called all the boys!"

"I'm sorry you won't be spending the night though," Tess said to her three friends, not wanting the fun to end yet.

"Says who?" Erin locked arms with her. "My mom stayed to help drive us over to your house."

"You mean you're coming over?" Tess's eyes grew big with excitement.

"We are!" Joann and Katie said at the same time.

This birthday wasn't a bust after all. "In that case," Tess said, "last one to the cars goes first for Truth or Dare! And I have something really awful in mind for anyone brave enough to choose Dare."

three

Bug Off

Friday Night, January 17

"Come on in my room, you guys." Tess led the way through the front door, down the hall, and into her bedroom. After flipping the switch that turned on both the radio and the light, she plopped down on her bed. "We can keep all the stuff in here and sleep in the family room."

"Cool room," Joann said. She smoothed her hand over Tess's Native American bedspread and looked admiringly at the glow-in-the-dark stars on the ceiling. "Especially the card." Joann giggled. She pointed at the orange card the class had made for Tess last October when she had burned her hand. Joann had organized making the card. Tess smiled back at her, glad that she had left it tacked on her bulletin board.

"Your mom cracked a lot of jokes at your party," Katie said.

"More pregnancy weirdness, I suppose," Tess said.

"I thought it was nice." Joann nudged Katie. Erin and Tess had grown close to the two other girls in the last few months. And Joann and Katie were each other's Secret Sisters, too.

"You guys, I have fabulous news," Katie burst out. "The roles for the school play were posted today, and guess who got Dorothy?"

"You?" Joann asked.

"Yes!" Katie squealed, and she and Joann jumped up and down holding hands.

"I just knew you would," Joann gushed. "You're such a good actress." A glint in Katie's eyes showed that she knew this to be true.

"Didn't you try out?" Joann turned toward Tess. "What part did you get?"

A flush of warmth swelled in Tess's chest, flooding red into her face. "I got cut."

"Oh. Sorry," Joann said.

"Maybe you can do makeup or something," Katie said.

"I'm not good with makeup."

"I'm sorry," Erin said, putting her arm around Tess. "I know how much you wanted a part."

"Yeah, a lot of good actors and actresses tried out this year," Katie said.

In other words, Tess thought, *someone with no talent, like me, didn't have a chance.*

"So what should we do?" Erin quickly changed the subject. "It's your birthday. We should do whatever you want."

"First, I'm going to make sure my mom keeps Tyler and Big Al out of the family room. It's off-limits to them tonight." Tess took off her jacket and with it tried to shake off a growing feeling of discomfort.

"Who's Big Al?" Katie asked.

"He's my brother's friend," Tess said. "Why don't you

guys pick up your sleeping bags and meet me in the family room? Erin knows the way."

"Okay," the others agreed. A few minutes later they had moved their gear in front of the TV.

Mrs. Thomas carried a large cardboard box into the family room. "Tess, a couple more presents to open; then I'll leave you girls alone."

She called, "Jim, Tess is opening her presents from your folks," and Tess's dad, Tyler, and Big Al joined them.

"How's my preteen?" Dad ruffled Tess's hair.

"Dad, that's so goofy. Don't call me that."

"Mind if we sit in on the action?" Tyler asked.

"As long as Hercules isn't breathing down my back," Tess said.

"What ho, old girl? He never breathes down your back. A little breath on the side of his cage, maybe. And besides, he has that sweet cricket breath."

"Yuck. Keep him locked up." Tyler's pet horned toad turned his back to Tess, nestling on the Hot Rocks inside his glass cage. She slit the packing tape on the side of the box and lifted three wrapped packages from inside.

"Open the big one first," Erin urged.

Tess did just that, pulling out a perfect pair of jean overalls from the package. "Yes!" she said, standing to hold them up against her.

"I don't know why a pretty young lady like you wants to wear painter's overalls." Her dad shook his head.

"Because they look great, and they're cool," Tess answered, already reaching for the second box.

"They are really nice," Katie agreed. "I wish I had some like that."

A second later more wrapping paper lay shredded on the family room carpet.

"Look, *The Ballad of Lucy Whipple!*" Tess lifted out a book by one of her favorite authors. Cracking it open, she inhaled deeply of the new book smell. She would start this tomorrow, after her friends went home.

"I never heard of that book," Joann said. "Have you?"

"No," Erin whispered.

"Well, everything she's written is really good," Tess defended.

"I say, what's in the third package?" Tyler eyed a small, rectangular box. Tess lifted it and shook it a little. A clicking, rattling noise came from inside.

"Sounds like some sort of spray paint," Tess said. "But why would Grandma and Grandpa send me that?" Unfolding a tiny card attached to the box, she read, "This is to keep away all the boys we're sure will be 'bugging' you now that you're growing into a beautiful young lady." She looked at her father, who seemed puzzled, too. Then she unwrapped the box.

"'Bug Off, the ultimate pest control,'" she read, turning pink. "Grandpa and his practical jokes." She laughed, embarrassed. Was he kidding? Beautiful? With her big feet and straggly hair? He must have sent this to the wrong granddaughter.

"Ho ho, can I see that?" Big Al grabbed for the can.

"Get away," Tess said, "before I exterminate Hercules."

"You wouldn't." Tyler protectively reached for his pet's cage.

"No, I wouldn't," Tess said, smiling at her brother. "Now we're going to change, and when we come back, you guys better be gone."

A few minutes later the girls returned to the family room.

"Good, I was afraid they might hang around like the pests they are." Tess sniffed.

"Want to watch a movie?" Erin asked.

"Okay. I brought my hair stuff," Joann said. "I could cornrow your hair."

"Oh yeah, definitely," Erin said. "Can I go first?"

"Well, let's do Tess's since it's her birthday."

"You're right." Erin blushed. "Sorry, Tess."

Tess leaned over to hug her friend. "Don't worry about it. And I really don't want my hair cornrowed."

"Why not?" Katie said. "It would look great."

Should she tell her secret? They were friends, after all. "Well, my ears are pretty big. It makes me feel self-conscious when my hair isn't covering them."

"Let's see." Katie pulled Tess's hair back from her face. "They're not that big. I wouldn't even have noticed if you hadn't said anything."

"It's not like you're Prince Charles or anything," Joann said.

Tess laughed. "I guess you're right. Ever since the Coronado Club drew a picture of me with huge ears on the bathroom mirror, I've felt really weird about them though."

"What happened?" Katie asked.

Erin looked at Tess, encouraging her to tell the story.

"Last summer I was really good friends with Colleen Clark. So when the school year started, I thought we would still be good friends. Was I wrong! She, Lauren, and Melody Shirowsky started the Coronado Club, and they wanted me to do some mean stuff to be initiated." Tess took a deep breath. "When I wouldn't do it, they drew a picture of me with huge ears on the bathroom mirror. It was so humiliating."

Katie and Joann looked just as mad as Erin had been when she found out. "Like they're perfect or something," Joann commented, and the others nodded in agreement.

"Okay, then, I'll do yours first," Joann said, and Erin settled down in front of her with a big plastic container of beads.

"Let's play Truth, Dare, Double Dare, Promise, or Repeat," Katie suggested. She smiled and raised her eyebrows as she slowly looked them in the eye. "Never say I'm not brave. So let's see your awful surprise, Tess. I'll go first. I pick Dare."

❋ four

Truth, Dare, Double Dare,
Promise, or Repeat

Friday Night, January 17

"This will be great." Tess jumped up, ran into the kitchen, and came back with a small plate.

"What's that?" Katie stared at the small brown slimy thing plopped in the center of the plate.

"It's an escargot. Otherwise known as a snail," Tess answered.

"Ooh, disgusting. What am I supposed to do with it?" Katie backed away from the plate.

"Eat it," Tess said. "My dad buys a whole bunch at New Year's Eve, when they're cheap, for parties and stuff."

"You're kidding. Oh, *why* did I pick Dare? I change my mind. I pick Truth."

"No way," Joann said. "A rule's a rule. Even for my best friend."

"I'll get sick. Who eats snails?" Katie moaned.

"It's a special treat in France. My dad likes them. He cooks them in garlic butter; so it's safe and everything."

"Well, here goes." Katie speared the tiny snail with a fork, plugged her nose, and gulped it down. The others stared at her, mesmerized, wondering if she would barf.

"Ooh, yuck." Erin plugged her nose. "Are you sick? Did it move? It isn't alive, is it?"

"It wasn't alive, was it?" Katie asked in a panic.

"No, it was dead," Tess reassured.

"Don't gross her out," Joann said, fingers spread over her eyes but still peeking out. "Maybe she'll throw up."

"Are you okay?" Tess asked. She didn't want Katie to get sick at her party.

"It wasn't too bad," Katie said bravely. "Not that I want to do it again. Now it's my turn. I pick Tess."

Tess answered, "Okay, I guess that's fair after I made you eat a snail! I pick Truth."

Katie took a swig of her root beer, washing down the snail trail, and asked, "What do you hate most about yourself?"

"I don't like my ears. Or any of my body too much. I wish I was smaller."

"Me, too," Katie said. "Like Erin. But artists are supposed to be different; so I guess I'm okay." Katie was great at art. Last month at the craft fair all of her painted pottery sold. Now with the starring role in the school play…Tess shook away the dark thoughts.

Joann said, "Erin, you do have nice skinny legs and stuff. A gymnast's body. Hey!" She snapped her fingers. "That reminds me. My gymnastics team is having tryouts for levels five and up. Why don't you try out?"

Erin cocked her head a little to look out of the corner of her eye, not wanting to jerk her hair away from Joann's practiced hands. "Thanks for inviting me, but I can't keep my balance on a beam. Besides, I'm really busy with my horses."

"I forgot you were so good with horses." Joann nodded her head.

"Actually, we're getting a new mare this month. And she's just had a foal!" Erin said, love of horses shining in her eyes. Tess noticed how pretty her friend was when excited.

"Oh great, you hadn't even told me!" Tess said. "Maybe I can come and ride her?"

"Well," Erin hesitated. "I think my grandpa wants only experienced riders on her for a while. You know, till we get used to her and she to us."

"Oh," Tess said, looking down. In other words, not inexperienced people like her. What was she good at anyway? A thought occurred to her, and she jumped up. "Maybe I could try out for gymnastics."

"*You?*" Joann asked, doubt written all over her face.

"Yes, me! I used to be in gymnastics in fourth grade. I even won a trophy. Want to see it?"

"Uh, no thanks," Joann said.

"Yeah, we believe you," Katie offered. Which meant they really didn't.

"But I did." Tess was steamed now. So she wasn't a great actress like Katie, or an experienced rider like Erin, or Junior Einstein like Joann. But she had done well in gymnastics, no matter what they thought. And she could do it again. Then she would be really good at something, too. Just like the others.

"I've seen her do cartwheels," Erin said. "They were perfect."

"This is a lot more than cartwheels," Joann said. "But I guess you can try out if you want."

Tess didn't think Joann sounded too enthusiastic. *She doesn't think I'm good enough. I'll show her.*

"I think I will," Tess said, a little mad now. "When are tryouts?"

"Practice is next Tuesday through Friday, and then tryouts are Saturday."

"I'll be there." She was determined to make that squad. Annoyed at Joann's doubt, Tess said, "Joann, you're next. Truth, Dare, Double Dare, Promise, or Repeat?"

Joann barely looked up from Erin's hair, fingers flying as they braided the strands of butterscotch blond hair, weaving beads in as she did. "I choose Promise."

"Um, let's see," Tess thought aloud.

"I have it," Erin said. "Joann, you have to promise to ask Kenny and Russell to show you how to dance the chicken."

"No way!" Joann said. "That would be more like Double Dare."

"A rule's a rule, remember," Katie reminded her. "And I think Kenny is cute."

"Cute? Are you joking?" Joann looked shocked. "Tess, do you have a thermometer? I think Katie is really sick."

"Ha ha," Katie answered. "You don't actually have to dance it; just ask them. Then you can run away."

"Okay," Joann agreed, giggling a bit. "I'll do it next week. Now it's your turn, Erin."

"Be brave," Tess teased.

"I pick Dare." Erin smiled at her Secret Sister.

"I have one," Katie said. "I dare you to put this makeup on, then go say good night to Big Al and Tyler." She handed over a Baggie with blush, lipstick, and eye shadow.

"Oh, Katie, more makeup?" Joann said. She hated makeup.

Smoothing a strand of hair, she finished the last of Erin's braids.

"It's just for play," Katie said. "I wouldn't wear it out in public or anything."

Tess winked encouragement at her friend. Erin brushed some on. Her face looked terrible—like a peacock's. Long blue streaks on her eyelids were set off with bright pink spots on her cheeks. A smear of Pretty in Pink lipstick marched across her mouth. She went down the hall to search for Big Al and Tyler. A few minutes later she returned.

"I couldn't find them, but I tried," she said, wiping the makeup off with a washcloth.

I wonder where they disappeared to, Tess thought. *They're usually more trouble.*

"You tried," Katie agreed. "Do you guys want to start a movie?"

"Sure. I'll get one from the closet before I make us a snack." Tess walked to the back of the room and opened the door to the closet where they stored their movies. She tugged on the door. "What's wrong with this thing?" After she gave it one last yank, the door flew open, and the two boys fell on top of one another on the floor. Big Al and Tyler were spying.

"Let's make tracks, old boy," Tyler shouted as they fled.

"You twerp!" Tess chased after them, gasping as she caught sight of the small, black electronic box in his hand.

Outgrown

Friday Night/Saturday Morning, January 17-18

"What's going on?" Mrs. Thomas walked into the kitchen, responding to Tess's scream.

"Look what those two are doing." Tess pointed toward Big Al's hand. "Look. A tape recorder."

Tyler rewound the tape a little and flicked it on. Katie's voice came across. "I think Kenny is cute." Tess glanced into the family room at Katie, who hid her head into a couch pillow in massive embarrassment.

"Were you recording the girls?" Mrs. Thomas asked them, lips pursed.

"Yeeesss, but we weren't going to do anything with it. We were just playing detectives. You know, Sherlock Holmes." Tyler squirmed.

"Hand it over." Mrs. Thomas held out her hand. "Detectives chase criminals, not twelve-year-old girls." She popped open the tape case and handed over the cassette to Tess.

"Say there," Tyler protested. "We have stuff on there, too."

27

Sandra Byrd

She nodded. "Tess, give Tyler the tape back after you've erased all of your conversations."

"Okay, Mom." Tess sniffed and turned to Tyler. "Get out of here before we hide Hercules and really give you something to look for." Turning back toward the family room, she motioned for Erin to come and help her with the popcorn and drinks.

"Here, check this out." Tess picked up a card in an already-opened envelope and tossed it. Erin pulled out the card and picture, and a letter fluttered to the floor.

"Who's this?" She stared at the picture.

"My beautiful, perfect, volleyball star cousin, Jane," Tess answered. "You don't have to read the letter, but it has one line of happy birthday to me, then a hundred lines about her latest achievements in sports and school. That's her team in the picture. She's the captain, and they're the state champions."

"Oh, that's nice," Erin said, setting down the card.

"No it's not!" Tess disagreed. "My grandparents called before dinner to tell me happy birthday and to see if the package got here. They spent practically the whole conversation talking about 'Jane this' and 'Jane that.' Nothing really about me."

"Oh, I'm sorry," Erin said. "That's no fun." She carried more drinks into the family room.

"They didn't have anything good to say about me since I never do anything as well as Jane," Tess mumbled to herself, shaking salt on the popcorn.

※

Tess always wondered why the night's events were called a sleepover. Nobody ever slept. After long hours of talking and watching movies, four groggy girls rose the next morning, rolled up sleeping bags, and gathered hair stuff. "My dad said he would be here by ten o'clock to pick up Katie and me," Joann said.

"Why are you leaving so early?"

"Gymnastics practice. I had a really great time though. Bowling was so cool. I hope we can do it again sometime."

"Yeah, and we'll have to have another Secret Sisters' Slumber," Katie said.

Joann's dad beeped his horn as he pulled up in front of the house. The two girls hugged Tess before leaving, then Tess shut the door and turned toward her own Secret Sister.

"What about you?" Tess asked Erin. "Are you leaving early, too?"

"I'm afraid so," Erin said. "I wish I could stay longer, but I promised to help out with the horses. Do you still want to come next week? We could pick you up. You could ride one of the other horses. My brother's coming since basketball is over." She elbowed Tess.

Tess smiled. Erin liked to tease Tess about her crush on Erin's brother Tom. He was two years older than the girls, and Tess thought he was the perfect guy. Cute, nice, and Christian. But she would never tell him that, of course.

"You know I'd love to come, but I'm going to try out for gymnastics, if my mom and dad let me. So I'll have to go to the practices."

"I didn't know you even liked gymnastics," Erin said. Although they felt as if they had known each other forever, Erin and Tess had only been friends since the beginning of the school year.

"I did in third and fourth grade. I quit when we moved here. The gym was far away." Which was true, but it was not like she had missed it a lot either.

"Well, okay. Maybe the week after—if you have time, that is." Erin's eyes dropped.

Tess felt confused. She loved riding with Erin. But now that she had said she was going to try gymnastics, she had to practice. Besides, maybe she would be really good at it.

"It's a deal. You'll pick me up for church tomorrow?" Tess put her arm around her friend.

"Yep, for sure." Erin's family picked up Tess each Sunday morning to take her to church with them. Tess had become a Christian last October. Although her parents weren't Christians, she hoped and prayed that they would love Christ, too, someday.

"Thank you for the calendar. I'm going to set it up right away. I'll read it first thing every day and think about you!" Tess said.

"Did you get much mail?" Erin asked, a twinkle in her eyes.

"Um, a couple of cards, a package from my grandparents, and Jane's letter. Why?"

"Just wondering." The doorbell rang, and when Tess opened it, her heart did a little flip. It was Tom.

"Hi, we're here for Erin." He smiled. "Happy birthday, Tess."

"Thanks." Tess blushed.

Erin picked up her gear and walked out. "See you tomorrow!"

Tess waved and then watched Erin's family drive away. Standing in front of her house for a minute, she surveyed the yard. Prickly pear cacti spread their spiky-skinned hands in a fan shape, waving good morning. On her way to the mailbox, she wandered over to the organ-pipe cactus and plucked out a couple of pieces of stray paper caught between its tubelike stems. Crumpling up the litter, she continued to crunch through the gravel to the mailbox.

Maybe she had some more birthday cards. Pulling down the mailbox door, she grabbed a handful. Wow! Was this all for her? Riffling through them she saw a pink envelope addressed to her and several postcards with free offerings for birthday kids. With a puzzled smile, she went back into the house.

"Mom," she bellowed, walking into the laundry room.

"Hi, honey. Are your friends gone?"

"Yes," Tess answered. "Look at all this mail! I got a couple of cards, and some free offers for ice cream, one for a hamburger, and one for a buy-one-get-one-free meal at Pizza Palace. Did you do this?"

Mom bent over the laundry basket, her stretch pants pulling tight over the place the baby grew. "Nope, I didn't. How fun. I wonder who did?"

"Look, here's one for the Christian bookstore. Two dollars off any book. I bet Erin did this! What a sweetie." Tess smiled. Wasn't it just like her sister to sign her up for all these?

Mom shut the lid to the washing machine as warm water rushed in and then turned to unload the dryer. "She's a good friend. I liked Joann and Katie, too."

"Yeah," Tess agreed. "Joann's gym is having tryouts for gymnastics. Practice is all this week and tryouts next Saturday. Can I go?"

"What? You?" Her mother straightened up.

"Yes, me," Tess said a little loudly. "Why does everyone have a hard time believing I can do gymnastics?"

"Hold on there, I didn't say that." Her mother folded a teal green bathroom towel end over end before continuing. "I haven't heard a peep about gymnastics in more than a year. Last I knew, you wanted drama lessons."

"Well, that's not going to work. I didn't even get a small part in the play," Tess said. "I know I can do gymnastics. I have before."

"You can already do lots of things," her mother said.

"But nothing really special, something I do really well. That others notice me for." Tess pleaded, "Maybe I'll get really good at it. Like Erin is really good with horses and Katie with art. And Joann with school and bowling and just about everything else. And," she said darkly, "cousin Jane."

"You'll get better on the horses with a little practice. Especially after you guys go to the dude ranch for camp this summer. You're good at lots of things, Tess. Why not do what you like?"

"I like gymnastics."

"I don't know. Let me think about it." Tess's mom took another towel and tossed it to her. "Why don't you help me fold these and then pick up that mess in the family room. Popcorn kernels are scattered all over the place." Tess folded the towel, then headed toward the family room.

She was sure her mother would come around. And Tess could always enlist her dad to help. He loved sports. "First," she said to herself, "I'll look for my leotard." The family room could wait.

After digging through a couple of messy drawers, she

located her midnight-blue leotard. She slipped off her jeans and struggled to pull on the leotard. No use. Peeling it off, she tossed it into the garbage. She could try out in shorts, but if she made the team, she would need to buy new leotards.

Glancing at her computer, she decided to log in to her prayer diary.

Dear Lord,

I had a really great birthday. Can you believe I'm twelve? I thought nobody was going to come to my slumber party, but then, surprise! And glow-in-the-dark bowling was so fun.

I'm thinking about trying out for gymnastics. Please help me make the team. Joann thinks I can't do it. But I know I can. I'll miss riding with Erin a lot. But I started to think about my new calendar. What does make a champion in life? I'm not really great at anything. Have you noticed? I mean, I'm okay at some stuff but not as much as I want to be. I can't think of anything besides gymnastics. When I tried on my leotard though, it didn't fit. I've outgrown it. Well, thanks for listening.

I love you, Tess

six

A Maestro
and a Zero

Sunday Evening, January 19

"Hurry! I want to get a good seat." Tess's mother practically ran down the auditorium aisle and squeezed herself into a center row. Tess and her father tagged along at a slower pace. When they finally caught up with Mrs. Thomas, she moved the purse and handbill she had set on the chairs to either side of her, saving their places.

"Do you think we'll have a good view?" Jim Thomas leaned over and asked his wife.

"I hope so. I've been looking forward to this all year. Haven't you?" she asked both her husband and Tess.

"Yes, definitely." Tess's father nodded his head enthusiastically.

"Um, yeah," Tess said. What else was she going to say? Her hand smoothed the red velvet upholstery of the seat, and she took a few minutes to glance around the concert hall.

High, curved ceilings adorned with sculptured, gold-kissed roses crowned the hall, meeting equally stunning walls draped with thick, damask curtains. A gleaming floor peeked from behind the heavy velour drapes pulled tight now to hide the musicians.

Honks, bleats, and warm-up scales emanated from the cloaked stage, and Tess glanced at her watch. Five minutes to go.

"I just can't wait!" Her mother squeezed Tess's hand. Tess loved Tyler, but she couldn't remember when she had seen her mother this excited over something Tess had done.

The heavy drapes swept open, and the youth orchestra sat poised, silent, onstage. Their conductor and teacher, Mr. Rosenblatt, spoke to the audience. "Ladies and gentlemen, in the rich and varied musical tradition of the state of Arizona, I present to you our youth orchestra!"

Everyone in the audience, including Tess, applauded loudly, standing up to encourage the musicians. A minute later the clapping died down, and Tess's mother whispered proudly, "I think Tyler is the youngest one there!"

After three or four selections, Tess heard her father catch his breath as Tyler played through his piano solo. She had heard it a thousand times before, on the spinet piano at home, but it never had sounded so vivid, so alive, as it did on the mahogany grand piano in the symphony hall.

After half an hour the performance came to a resounding close. Tess's mother wiped her eyes when Tyler stood up, looking like a baby penguin in his tiny tuxedo, to take a bow. He seemed so small on that big stage next to the giant piano and with the rest of the orchestra to his side.

"My goodness. We have a maestro," Jim Tyler said, pride gleaming in his eyes.

Yep, Tess thought. *A maestro, Tyler, and a zero, me.*

seven

Out with the Old, In with the New

Monday, January 20

The bright fluorescent lights of the sixth-grade science area bore down on the girls as they worked. "Did you do the math assignment yet?" Erin asked, mixing baking powder into warm water and watching the chemical reaction. Bubbles frothed up and down the side of the bowl.

"Yes, how about you?" Tess said. Science was her favorite part of the day—the week maybe. Definitely the most interesting subject in school.

"No, I didn't understand the last half. I kept reading it over and over and still couldn't figure it out. Every time I looked up the answers in the back of the book they were different than mine. I guess I'll ask Ms. M. at recess. I can't seem to get it," Erin finished glumly.

"I'll stay in to help you," Tess said.

"Thanks." Erin measured a little more powder into the cloudy water while Tess read the gas gauge.

"I forgot to thank you for all the cool stuff you signed me up for. Like the burgers and the book coupon and stuff," Tess said.

"Oh, you're welcome. I wished I had more money to buy you a better present, but since I didn't, I thought if I signed you up for all those freebies that would be like more presents."

"Maybe we could go to the mall next week and use some of the coupons. I'm going today, but it's just a mom-'n-me thing." Tess rolled her eyes. "My mom says we don't have enough time together."

"My mom tells me the same thing. Let's plan it next week." Erin read the gas gauge. "Nine-point-five."

Tess scribbled the number down on their log. "Did you see Michelle's new haircut?"

"Yes, it's really cute, isn't it? It would look good on you, too, Tess."

"Actually, I was thinking that. If it weren't for my ears."

"I still think it would look cute," Erin said.

"Are you ladies doing okay?" Ms. Martinez, their sixth-grade teacher, walked up behind them.

"Yes," they said in chorus. Ms. M. smiled, her tan skin taut over high cheekbones. Her long black hair, clasped by a silver lightning-bolt clip, tumbled down her back.

"I'll check on the boys then." She moved on.

"That reminds me, isn't Joann supposed to ask Kenny and Russell to show her how to do the chicken?" Erin giggled.

"Yes," Tess responded. "Let's remind her. Oh, Joann…," she sang out, walking over to the table where Joann and Katie worked on their experiment.

"Hi," Joann said.

"Don't forget what you're supposed to ask Kenny and Russell today," Erin reminded her.

"Oh yeah," Joann said, slowly removing her science goggles. "Well, never say I was a 'chicken.'" The other three girls groaned at the bad joke, then Joann walked over to Kenny and Russell.

Tess, Erin, and Katie leaned over the table to see and hear better.

"Excuse me," Joann started.

"Why? Did you burp?" Kenny asked, grinning and chucking Russell on the arm. Cracking up, Russell moved closer, waiting to see what Joann would say.

"Could you teach me how to do the chicken dance?" she finished. Dumbfounded, Kenny and Russell stared at her. "Oh, never mind," she said, running back to her table.

"I did it!" she said triumphantly. Erin and Tess giggled, and Katie's face was red from holding laughter inside.

After pausing a minute to recover from her giggle fit, Joann asked Tess, "Are you still coming to practice tomorrow?"

"Yes. I'm going shopping after school today to see if I can find some leotards."

"You can try out in shorts, you know," Joann said.

You mean, since I won't make the team, Tess thought. "I'll need some for regular practices," Tess said. "Besides the team's leotard, that is." She smiled inside, already envisioning Joann's surprised reaction when she saw that Tess really was good.

"Right," Joann quickly added. "I'll write down the gym address later. You'll have to pay the fifty-dollar registration fee up front."

Oh-oh. She hadn't asked her parents about paying any fee. Time enough to worry about that later.

At that, Tess and Erin returned to their baking-soda stew, hoping to finish in time to look over the new magazine Tess had brought to school.

※

"I don't have much time, Tess. I have an advertisement to finish writing this afternoon, and Tyler can only stay with Big Al a short time. Where should we go?" Mrs. Thomas asked as she jerked the car into second gear and pulled away from Big Al's house.

"How about the Saguaro Mall?"

Her mother nodded absentmindedly. "What are we going for again?"

"Leotards! Mom, don't you remember? Gymnastics?"

"Oh yeah. Sorry. I have my mind on work a lot lately and, of course, the little one," her mother patted her tummy affectionately. "I need to stop by the music store to buy some more piano music for Tyler, too. His teacher called in the order. Wasn't his recital wonderful? I never would have imagined I'd have such a musically gifted child!" Molly Thomas smiled affectionately.

Well, we know it's not me, Tess thought. *I'm already losing out to the baby, and it's not even born yet!*

"You are going to come to my practices, aren't you?" Tess suspected her mom never imagined she would have such a gymnastically gifted child either.

"I'll come to at least one and the tryouts," her mother answered. "Of course, if you make the team, we'll come to all the meets."

Tess nodded in satisfaction. Then the spotlight would be on her for a change.

"Don't you want to look at some other clothes?" her

mom asked. "Are you sure you want to spend this money on leotards? We can buy leotards if you make the team."

"Why doesn't anyone think I'm going to make the team?" Tess wailed. "Nobody believes in me."

"It's not that, Tess," her mother explained as they parked the car. "It's just that you haven't mentioned gymnastics in so long, and now suddenly you want to be on a team again."

"Well, I've been adjusting to a new school and making new friends. It's not like you guys were likely to drive me to the old gym after we moved, and I hadn't heard of any good ones on this side of town." Tess abruptly changed the subject. "Where should we go first?"

"How about getting a lemonade, then Tyler's music, and then Robinsons-May?" her mother suggested.

"I could use something to drink," Tess agreed. After a girl wearing a yellow beanie served them two cherry lemonades, they sipped the drinks together.

"Ready to shop?" her mom asked. "I have to pick up Tyler by four-thirty."

"Yes." They walked to the very end of the mall to pick up Tyler's music before meandering back to Robinsons-May. Tess smiled as she passed the cosmetics booths where several sales associates were applying fresh make-up to women of all ages. No wonder Katie liked makeup; it was like painting!

"Would you like to try our new fragrance?" A lady with big, yellow hair blocked Tess and her mother as they tried to navigate the aisle.

"Sure." Mrs. Thomas smiled. The lady sprayed each of their wrists with a fruity, vanilla fragrance.

"Mmm, that's sort of nice," Tess said, surprised. She

didn't usually wear perfume. Well, sometimes Love's Baby Soft, but that didn't count.

"Would you like one of our sample flasks?" the lady offered.

"Okay," Tess's mother said. The lady offered them each one, and Mrs. Thomas handed hers to Tess.

"Why don't you give this one to Erin, and then you can be the Secret Scented Sisters?" she said.

"Good idea, Mom." Tess tucked them into her purse. "We're so mature now, we need ladies' perfume." She batted her eyelashes in mock maturity, and they shared a giggle. As soon as they arrived in the athletic-wear department, Tess ran to look at the leotards.

"I'll look over here; you look over there," she called to her mother.

Tess pushed aside several leotards, searching for one that might look nice. Some of them had high-cut legs, which she didn't like, or belts that might pinch.

"How about this one?" her mother held up a selection.

"No thanks, it's the color of Grey Poupon," Tess said.

Her mother laughed. "Yes, it does remind you of mustard, doesn't it?"

"This one looks like Space Warriors," Tess muttered. "Can we try another store?"

"I'm sorry. We really don't have time," her mother explained. "It took me longer to get Tyler's music than I thought."

"I thought this trip was for me!" Tess complained.

"I'm sorry, Tess, but other people have things they need, too. We'll come back another day."

"I guess I'll just wear shorts to try out, and we can look

somewhere else next Monday after the team is formed." Tess tried not to be upset as they headed toward the exit.

"Sorry, honey. We'll try again." On the way toward the door, they walked past the Ladies' Essentials department.

"Let's stop here," her mother suggested. "It won't take too long."

"Why? Do you need something?" Tess felt even less important now that the shopping trip had turned into a buying excursion for everyone but her—and her dad, of course, who wouldn't care that he wasn't included.

"Yes," Mrs. Thomas answered, "but I was also thinking you might need some items. You are a young lady now, you know."

"Me?" Tess didn't pretend she hadn't given it any thought, but she hadn't actually approached her mother about buying anything.

"Sure, let's see what they have. We'll squeeze it into five minutes." They walked over to the Beautiful Beginnings section, and Mom sorted through the racks. "This bra is pretty. White lace with embroidered roses. Looks comfy."

"Sure, it looks okay," Tess said. It was dainty and feminine. It just didn't seem as if she was old enough to be thinking about this yet. "I didn't realize throwing away my leotard would lead to this!" She giggled nervously.

"Out with the old, in with the new," her mother said. "You are mature now, remember." Her mom batted her eyelashes like Tess had with the perfume, and they giggled again.

"May I help you?" A tidy, older woman approached.

"I think we're doing okay," Tess's mother answered.

"May I measure the young lady?" Before Tess or her mother could answer, the saleswoman whipped off the neon yellow tape measure hanging from her neck like a stethoscope. "Arms up, please," she instructed, and Tess looked at her mother, who nodded.

Holding up her arms like a scarecrow or a large, awkward bird, Tess didn't dare look down at the measurement.

"There you are, dear. Now we'll get the right size. Here." She swept her arm toward a particular size on a metal rack. "Any one of these will do. Why don't you choose some, and I'll meet you at the cash register."

"Go ahead, honey. Pick out two or three. I'm going into the maternity section, and I'll meet you at the register in a minute or two." Her mother raced a few rows over.

Now that the embarrassing part was over, Tess enjoyed the idea of picking out a couple of bras. "Hmm, maybe a sports bra," she said.

Just then, out of the corner of her eye, she saw something horrible. Rather, someone horrible. Kenny, the class clown, was in the young men's department just across the aisle. Oh no! Had he seen her being measured? What if he saw what she was buying? Could she make it to the checkout stand and get the bras in the bag before he saw her?

※ eight

Sideline

Tuesday, January 21

Amazingly, the next morning at school passed quickly
with no comment from Kenny. Not even a sidelong look
at her or a knowing chuckle. Tess breathed easier. He
must not have seen her yesterday.

"What's for lunch?" Erin asked, sliding alongside Tess
in the cafeteria line.

"I don't know yet," Tess answered. "I hate it when my
tray and silverware are all wet. It's gross." She snatched
an extra napkin from the dispenser to wipe down her
tray.

"Well, whatever it is, it smells good." Erin nudged her
along. "Hurry up; I'm hungry!"

"You're always hungry." Tess laughed. She chose a
plastic-wrapped sandwich, a mini-bag of chips, and an
orange. Erin chose the same but added a chocolate-chip
cookie to hers.

"Don't you want a cookie?"

"Nope. I'm trying to skinny down for gymnastics."

"You're not fat! I think you look just fine," Erin encouraged. "But if you don't want your cookie…"

"I'll take it for you," Tess said, plopping the cookie on her tray. "Let's sit down."

"I can't wait until it's our turn to paint the mural," Erin said. "Do you still want to try out for the mural team next month?" Each sixth-grade class painted a wall of the cafeteria before they moved on to middle school.

"I don't know. It depends on how busy I am with gymnastics."

"Oh. I was hoping we might do it together." Neither of them voiced their real fear, but it was there, sneaking around the spoken conversation. What if Tess didn't have time to do much of anything with Erin?

"Did you notice anything, um, different about me today?" Tess quickly changed the subject.

"Nooo…" Erin studied her friend's face. "Not new clothes. I saw those overalls at your party."

"Not the overalls, but it is new clothes. Clothes you can't see." Tess pointed to the shoulder strap beneath her shirt and whispered, "I got a bra."

"Oh wow! When did that happen?" Erin said with real surprise.

"Yesterday, at the mall with my mom." Tess bit into her turkey sandwich, chewing slowly to savor each bite. Was she going to have to eat like an ant from now on?

"That's so exciting! Do you feel older?" Erin smiled at her friend.

"Well…" Tess thought for a minute. "I do. Yep, I do."

"I didn't know you were planning to do that," Erin said a

bit wistfully. "I don't think I need one yet. Maybe my mom will take me anyway."

"I wasn't planning. It was more like spur of the moment. Anyway, it almost turned into a disaster!"

"How?" Erin leaned closer, polishing off her chips and reaching for the first cookie.

"Well, I was just standing there almost ready to pay, when I saw Kenny right across the aisle from me!"

"No!" Erin said, aghast. "Did he see you?"

"I guess not." Tess smiled. "I sort of hid in the displays, then sneaked up to the cashier. He didn't say anything to me today, and I know he would have."

"That was a close one," Erin agreed. A sad look stole across her face.

"What's the matter?" Tess said.

"Oh, I don't know. It's silly."

"No it's not! I won't think anything you tell me is silly," Tess reassured. "Do you want to tell me outside?"

"Maybe. In private." Erin scanned the crowded lunchroom. They pitched their trash into the can and walked outside. A chilly wind blew swirls of dead leaves through the schoolyard. Most students chose to stay inside today. Except for a few boys tossing a ball and a roadrunner scampering alongside the playground, the girls were alone. Tess pulled her sweat jacket more tightly around her, and Erin pulled down her sleeves. Taking refuge in a corner, they sat down.

"I just feel as if we're doing a lot of separate stuff lately. You know, like gymnastics. And then, you know, this." Erin pointed at Tess's shoulder, referring to her purchase yesterday.

"I know what you mean," Tess said. "But we can still do lots of things together."

"Yeah," Erin said. "And I think it's great you're doing gymnastics since you really want to. So don't feel bad. I just want to tell you how I feel."

"Thanks." Tess wrapped her arms around Erin in the silence, another chill wind cutting through her heart from the inside. Why was she so uncomfortable every time she thought about gymnastics? Didn't she believe she would make it either? Did she really want to do gymnastics like Erin assumed? She needed to stand out at something, and it sure wasn't drama or horses or volleyball or music.

After school that day Erin and Tess walked out together. "I'll call you tonight," Tess said.

"Okay, I'll be praying for your practice." Erin headed toward her car with her brother Josh. Tess stepped into the Jeep with Tyler and her mother.

"I don't understand why I have to go to this rinky-dink gymnastics practice," Tyler muttered as they drove away.

"Because we're taking Tess and waiting for her. Tomorrow we'll drop her off, and Joann's dad will take her home." Molly Thomas jerked the car into gear and roared out of the parking lot, narrowly missing several parked cars. Tess glanced at Tyler, who raised his eyebrows, then covered his eyes with his hands.

"What are you doing?" Mrs. Thomas asked, glancing at him in the rearview mirror.

"I don't want to be a witness to my own death," he said.

"Oh, Tyler," his mother said, "my driving isn't that bad."

Tess didn't agree with her, but hunkered down in the seat until they arrived at the gym a few minutes later.

"Why don't you run in and explain why you're here? I'll buy Tyler a drink. Then we'll come sit on the sidelines," her mother suggested.

"Okay." Tess hauled her bag out of the car and walked up to the front desk. After nervously tapping on the glass to get the receptionist's attention, she explained, "I'm Tess Thomas, Joann Waters's friend. She invited me to practice this week and for level-five tryouts on Saturday."

"Do you have any previous gymnastics experience?" the receptionist asked.

"Yes, I was on a level-four team at Hang Time, two years ago." Tess named her old gym.

"Oh, okay then. Why don't you go change, and I'll explain it to the coach, Stefani. Meet her at the mats."

Tess took her bag into the changing room. Several girls about Tess's age giggled and talked together as they dressed. One girl French-braided her friend's hair. Self-conscious, Tess began to change. Nobody came over to introduce herself, although a few glanced Tess's way. Where was Joann? Tess headed out to the gym.

Thick blue mats covered the floor, except for the bleachers and entrance-exit areas. In one corner the bars were stretched several feet off the floor. A flouring of hand chalk dusted the mats beneath them. It had been a long time since Tess had swung herself up and around the parallel bars. Her mind thumbed through all of the moves she used to do, reaching to call them into her current memory. Come on, Tess, this is your big chance.

After the bars, she walked farther over toward the wall where the horse sat. In front of it stood the springboard. She didn't have to be experienced with this horse, she thought. Her legs folded into a lotus position on the mat, and she gently stretched her muscles, pulling an arm over her head. Joann walked up.

"Hi! I'm glad you came." She seemed genuinely pleased, and Tess smiled back. "You'll like Stefani," Joann continued. "She's really nice, but she works you hard."

"Oh, like how?" Tess asked.

"Well, one time I asked her why I wasn't able to do some of the things that the level-eight girls were doing, and she said if I didn't goof around so much and concentrated, I probably could. I'm trying out for level eight this week."

Goof off? Joann? Tess couldn't imagine intense Joann goofing off. "You're trying out for level eight?" Tess said, aghast. She had assumed Joann was trying for level five or possibly six.

"Yep. I've been at it a long time," Joann said with pride.

Great, something else to be shown up in, the very thing Tess had chosen to excel in. As she scanned the gym, she saw focus and concentration on even the smallest face. These girls took this sport seriously.

"Anyway, I'd better get back to the beam," Joann said. "I'll talk to you later!" She waved. Tess's heart sank as she watched Joann walk back to the balance beam with a grace and purpose Tess didn't feel. Glancing over at the bleachers, she saw her mother and Tyler, his face buried in a comic book.

For just a second Tess wished she could sit on the sidelines, too. What if she failed at this, too?

nine

Practice Number Two

Wednesday, January 22

The second day at practice was easier than the first. As Tess changed into her shorts, one girl nodded at her, and another came over to talk with her.

"Hi. You're new here, aren't you?"

"Yeah," Tess answered. "I just started coming to practice. I'm trying out for the level-five team this weekend."

"Nice to meet you. My name is Amy." Tess recognized her from the level-five team she had seen working out yesterday. Tess nodded back at her and smiled before she finished dressing.

Standing in front of the mirror, she slowly pulled the brush through her hair. Yesterday Stefani had mentioned that Tess would need to pull it back; loose hair wasn't allowed. Tess had brought a scrunchie and now pulled her hair into a tight ponytail. She wiggled her head back and forth, watching the hair move. First from the left, then from the right she examined her ears. They were big. But no one seemed to be pointing or even looking at them. It sure would be nice to have one of those cute, short bobs like the gymnasts on TV. The girls with small ears, she reminded herself. Smoothing on some lip gloss before closing the locker, she prepared to go.

Lots of others were out on the soft blue mats today, even more than yesterday. They weren't all trying out for teams. Some were just there to practice or were working on other levels. But a lot of people were there for tryouts. Tess knew just by talking with them.

As she stood in line for the bars, she fixed her eyes on the blonde girl in the pink leotard ahead of her. Once mounted, the girl spun so fast so many times she looked like pink thread winding around a bobbin. Suddenly she stopped, holding still on her stomach before firmly dismounting, one arm raised in triumph. A little ball of doubt burned in Tess's stomach. No way was she that good.

"That was nice," Tess managed to say as the girl moved aside to let Tess mount the bars.

"Thanks," the girl smiled. Tess noticed how small, lithe, and thin the girl was.

"I'm trying out for level five," the girl continued. "How about you?"

"Me, too," Tess said. Could that be right? This girl seemed so much younger than Tess. And really good. Don't compare yourself to others all the time, she remembered her mother saying. Just have fun.

"Well, good luck," the girl said, moving toward the balance beam.

"Thanks," Tess said. "I'll need it."

But Tess surprised herself. Once she warmed up on the bars, she didn't do as badly as she had thought. She spun around, gripping the bars with strength. She liked the feel of the air as it rushed past her head, free and clean and cool. It had been so long since she had pulled back her hair, she had forgotten how fresh the air felt on sweaty skin. The bars had always been Tess's favorite. This was fun! When she firmly dismounted and raised her hands in the air, she had the feeling she just might make the team after all.

ten

Dreamy Draw

Wednesday Evening, January 22

Later that evening, as Tess stretched her muscles before hiking, she heard her father ask, "Are you ready to go?"

"Yes, but I'm tired, Dad," she said.

"I know. We'll just go for a little hike. I've missed spending time with you. And even though you're working on gymnastics, you need to work on hiking, too, if you want to do the Rim-to-Rim." Her father double-knotted his laces, and they headed up the Dreamy Draw.

Not far up the crunching gravel, Tess began to tire. The sun was setting early; few other hikers were out on this cool winter evening. The birds that usually whistled while Tess and her dad walked had long ago returned to their homes to nestle for the night. A lonely night bird called in the far distance, and the evening breeze picked up slightly. The sun sent its final red splashes, and the advancing dusk filtered down through the last layer of day. A multiarmed saguaro cactus cast a dark, bold shadow on one side of the trail; the shadow looked like an octopus flattened on a sandy sea floor. Somewhere farther up the trail a team of bullfrogs croaked, hiding in the tall rye grass, no doubt.

After fifteen minutes, Tess said, "Can we sit down for a while?"

"Tired out, huh?" her father asked.

Tess nodded, and they found a long, smooth stone to use as a bench.

"How was gymnastics?"

"It was good. Before I started, I thought it would be no problem, but then after yesterday I thought I was really bad. After I got back into the swing of things though, it started to come back to me. And the coach is nice." She pulled her watchband away from her wrist and scratched at a bug bite.

"I'm glad. You know I think sports are really important. But you're growing up now; you're going to be faced with more and more activities. You'll have to sort through them. Like this." Her dad waved toward the trail. "Are you going to drop out of hiking if you make the team?"

"No, I love hiking!" Tess said. Hiking, and time alone with her father while doing it, were really important to her. "I'm sure after I get back up to speed I can handle both."

"We'll see. And your mother is going to need some help after the baby comes, you know." A troubled look crossed her father's face. Even in the dim evening light Tess saw it.

"What is it, Dad?" Tess asked.

"Well—" he hesitated a minute. "I guess now that you're growing up, you can handle it."

Tess picked at a hangnail while she waited for him to continue.

"Mom went to have a test a bit ago. It's called an amniocentesis, and it tells if the baby is healthy or sick—usually with Down syndrome. Most women have this kind of test if they are pregnant after they are thirty-five years old. The test results come back next week, and I was just thinking about the baby. And Mom. That's all."

"Oh." Tess sat quietly, looking at the stars emerging from the darkening night. She remembered who made the stars and felt some reassurance.

"I think it'll be all right, Dad. You know, God is in charge." The last statement was bold, considering her dad's disinterest in Christianity and God in general. But she really felt it was true.

Her father leaned over and ruffled her hair. "You know, Tess, you might be right. Maybe you could remember to pray about that."

"I will, Dad, I will." Tess smiled to herself. Yippee! Her dad had never asked her to pray for something before.

"And now, we had better get back." Mr. Thomas picked up his canteen and turned toward the trailhead.

"We didn't get very far," Tess said sheepishly. If she hadn't been so tired, they might have finished. If she hadn't been at practice, they might have started earlier.

"It's okay. Just remember what I said about choices," her father said. "And I'll bet you have homework to do."

"I do," she agreed, and they turned back toward the car.

She had taken only a few steps when she felt a hot stab of pain in her ankle as she fell. "Help!"

Her dad, just a few paces behind her, ran forward. "Are you okay?" He grabbed her arm to help her up, but when she tried to stand, she almost collapsed.

"No, I don't think so! What's happening?" she cried, her tongue thick with the gritty taste of the dust she had kicked up. Hot pokers of pain shot through the tendons in her ankle and crept up her leg like a poisonous vine.

"Let's see." Her dad sat down on the ground beside her and gently felt her ankle. "Can you move it?"

"A little." She gently twirled her ankle and then bit her lip as another spike of pain reached up her calf.

"I think you have a twisted ankle. Hopefully not sprained," he said. "You must have stepped into a snake hole." He shook his head. "I should have known better than to come when it was this dark."

"Don't be upset, Dad," Tess offered. "We had to come late because of my practice. So it's my fault."

"Let's not worry about that now. Let's just get you back to the car."

Tess nodded, then leaned on her father and hobbled down the hill. She tried not to cry. Ruined. Her chances at gymnastics were now zero.

An hour later Tess sat down at her desk, supposedly to start her homework. She could barely keep her eyes open after her hot shower. Warm vanilla milk steaming from a mug on her desk made her even sleepier. But her throbbing ankle kept her awake. So, closing her school folder, she logged in to her computer diary instead and began typing.

Dear Jesus,

A terrible thing happened tonight. I know you already saw it. My ankle is twisted. It's not too swollen. So I don't think it's sprained, but Mom wrapped it in a bandage anyway. I guess this probably kills my

Double Dare

chances at gymnastics. I'll show up tomorrow and see what Stefani says. What a joke. I might as well quit trying to find anything I'm special at.

"Oh, no! I forgot to call Erin!" Tess checked her watch before continuing.

But it's too late. She's going to think I forgot about her. We talk every night! How am I going to do all this?
Thanks for reminding me about you when I looked at the stars. It's so cool how you can remind me of yourself with the eensiest-teensiest things every day.

Love, Tess

She limped across the room to pick up her clothes from the floor, yawning as she did so. Obviously, she was too tired to do homework. As she placed her new bra in the top drawer, she thought about how Dad said she was growing up. Had Mom told him about their little shopping trip? A warm flush spread on her face. Getting older was a lot of fun, but it could be awkward, too.

eleven

Balancing Truth

Thursday, January 23

"I say, old girl, what are you doing?" Tyler looked quizzically at her. Tess took dainty steps through the kitchen, arms out to her side. Grandpa Pat's big Bible was balanced on top of her head.

"Is that a new spiritual exercise your church makes you do?" her dad asked.

Tess was about to protest when she looked up and caught the twinkle in his eye. "No, Dad." She grinned. "I'm working on keeping my balance for the beam. This way I can make lots of different moves and correct myself if I move too quickly or crookedly. Some of the other girls do it, too." She marched around the room a couple of more times, squatting without dropping the book, rounding corners, and keeping her balance. Her ankle was weak, and she wobbled as she walked, but she kept at it. Each time she held her head up, she smiled with satisfaction. She was making progress.

"I've heard that, too," her mother agreed, munching popcorn out of a well-worn plastic bowl. Picking up the pace, Tess pulled open the freezer. A blast of stale frozen mist sprayed her face.

"Pee-yew." She backed away.

"I guess I'd better clean the freezer, huh?" her mother asked.

Tess nodded. Mom meant well, but she didn't exactly keep a spotless home.

"I think it's the shrimp I got on sale last month," her mother mused to herself. "I'm just too tired to do much cleaning. I remember being tired when I was pregnant with you and with Tyler, but I don't remember it lasting this long." She glanced up and asked Tess, "What are you looking for?"

"Ice cream. Don't we have any chocolate-chip mint?"

"Ho there, old girl. Sorry to disappoint, but Big Al and I polished it off after school." Tyler licked his lips, and Tess glared at him.

"Isn't anything safe from you two? Al doesn't even live here. Why does he scarf down all our good food? Last week it was the chips. Last month it was both boxes of macaroni and cheese."

"I say, we're doing you a favor. Aren't you supposed to be slimming down? Gymnasts don't devour big bowls of ice cream."

Tess flipped the Bible off her head and grabbed a Popsicle.

"Speaking of that, how did practice go today?" her dad asked.

"Okay. Stefani was pretty bummed about the ankle but said it didn't mean I'd have to drop out." Tess didn't want to even think about that. Another chance! "She did say I'd have to be much more careful. And that it might be harder to make the team."

Mrs. Thomas asked, "What do you think your chances are?"

"Really great. I'm making fast progress. Stefani said so," Tess happily reported.

Stefani was a tough coach. They called her Mighty Mouse when she was out of earshot. She was energetic and small. But she worked the girls hard. And Stefani had said Tess was progressing—at least until she hurt her ankle.

"I'm going to do my homework," Tess said to no one in particular.

"Please pick up the dirty clothes in the bathroom," her mother called after her.

"Oh, all right." Why couldn't her mom do it herself? Tess wondered, suddenly tired. Wasn't that what mothers were for? Tess certainly had enough to do. She was behind on her homework, and she was worn out. Ever since her mother got pregnant, it seemed she couldn't do half the stuff she used to. She had energy to paint the baby's room though. With stars. Tess hoped this kid wasn't going to be the star of the family.

After tossing several orphan socks and a pair of inside-out jeans into the hamper, she walked into her room and shut the door. Flipping on the CD player, she flopped down on her bed, finishing the Popsicle and trying to get motivated to do her homework.

"Hi, girl." Tess swished her finger in Goldy's bowl. Tess's chubby fish wagged her tail as she circled in her slightly slimy water.

Tess tapped in some food. "There you go. Sorry I forgot

you this morning." Spying the calendar that Erin had given her, Tess realized she had been too busy to flip the days and keep it current.

She turned to January 23 and read, "Psalm 139:13-14: You made my whole being; You formed me in my mother's body. I praise you because you made me in an amazing and wonderful way. What you have done is wonderful. I know this very well."

That seemed like a good verse. Did it mean anything special for her?

Tess snapped her fingers and jumped up. Grabbing a piece of scented paper from her stationery box, she knew just what this was meant for. It would be the perfect verse to write down for her mother. Then, if Mom worried about whether the new baby was okay, she could just look at that verse and see the truth. The Bible always told the truth, the whole truth, and nothing but the truth.

A few minutes later Tess had swirled the verse on the paper with a gold calligraphy pen and set it aside to dry. She would give it to her mom tomorrow or maybe later tonight.

The phone rang. "Hello?" Tess answered it quickly, before Tyler could get to it.

"Hi, it's me," Erin said. "I missed talking last night. So I thought I'd call you this time."

"Good idea," Tess said. A wide gulf of busyness separated the sisters this week.

"How did practice go today?"

"Stefani, the coach, said I could still try out, even with my ankle."

"Are you sure that's safe?"

"I guess so. I'm not quitting now. Not when it's my big

chance, even if it's not safe." Tess changed the subject. "How's riding?"

"Really good. The mare and foal arrived. My brothers and I get to name them."

"No! That is so great!"

"I know," Erin agreed, and Tess could hear the joy in her friend's voice.

Tess longed to ride again. She had just been getting good, and she and Erin shared so many fun times, secrets, and plans on their rides. Plus, they were going to the Lazy K Bar camp this summer to better their riding skills. "When can we ride again?"

"How about next week?" Erin asked. "How about Tuesday? Do you want to come home with me from school, and we can go over to my grandma and grandpa's house together?"

"I'll ask my mom," Tess said. She really wanted to go. But what about gymnastics? Once she made the team, practice was every day after school for two hours, plus Saturdays.

"And," Erin continued, "I have another surprise."

"What is it?"

"You'll have to see tomorrow." Erin giggled. "I better go. I finished my math homework but haven't done any health yet."

"Me either," Tess said. "I'll see you in the morning. Don't forget it's Funky Friday."

"I won't," Erin agreed. They had decided that each Friday they would dress according to a theme. One week they wore all green, because Tess's mother was Irish-American, and one week they wore western wear. This week they chose funky clothes.

"I'd better go raid my mom's closet." Tess giggled.

"See you tomorrow," Erin said before hanging up.

A rush of warmth ran through Tess as she hung up the phone. Erin was such a good friend. A real sister. Wouldn't it be a blast to go riding next week and see the new mare? She would have to figure out how she could do it. Maybe miss one practice or something. But even as she thought it, she knew in her heart Stefani wouldn't allow her to miss a minute.

✳ twelve

Cafeteria Ladies

Friday, January 24

"Cool outfit." Erin admired Tess's fringed shirt. "Very funky."

"You, too. Bead-o-mania." Tess giggled, rubbing her fingers over Erin's orange bead necklace.

"How's the project coming, girls?" Ms. Martinez walked over to their art table.

"Fine," Erin said. "I'm just choosing the acrylics I want to paint my plate with."

"What kind of plate will it be?" Ms. M. asked.

"A 'special day' plate. Whoever has a birthday or wins a game, or whatever, can eat dinner off of it. My mom saw one in the store," she continued, "but it cost too much. So I wanted to make one."

"What a good idea!" Ms. M. said. "What are you making, Tess?"

"A vase for my grandma."

"That's nice! I made a vase, too. I'm going to dry my wedding flowers and put them in it after my wedding."

"Ooh!" both girls said.

"Are you getting excited?" Tess asked. "It's in April, right?"

"Yes." Ms. M. smiled before adding, "Don't forget your good-deed project is today. You signed up to help in the cafeteria." Each person in the class did a good deed for the school. The students in Ms. M.'s class could either clean up the playground or help in the cafeteria.

"Oh, I totally forgot!" Tess said. "Did you remember?"

"No," Erin admitted, "but that's okay. Do we work all four lunch periods?"

"Yes. I'll excuse you at the first lunch period. Report to Mrs. Steadman in the cafeteria."

After Ms. M. left, Tess said, "Do you mind if I invite Heidi to do art with us?"

"Um...no," Erin said. "I guess not. If she hasn't gone to her special classes."

Tess scanned the room and saw Heidi tapping lightly on the pet rat cage. "She's still here."

"I don't mind or anything, but, ah, why do you want to invite her? I mean, we never have before," Erin said.

"Well, I've been thinking about her. 'Cause my mom had a special test to see if our new baby has Down syndrome."

"What did it say?"

"The results haven't come back yet." Tess smoothed her pottery with a mini-sandpaper filer.

"Oh," Erin said. "Go ahead and invite her."

Tess walked over and asked Heidi to work with them. But Tess came back alone.

"Didn't she want to come over?"

"She said in a little bit. She was still watching the rats," Tess said. "But I think she was happy I asked her.

"I was thinking, maybe God balances it all out," Tess continued. "You know, some people seem to have a lot of things, like they're rich or popular or cute or something. But then they're really rude. Or stuck up."

"Like Lauren and Colleen," Erin added.

"Exactly," Tess agreed. "Take you. Math is hard for you, but you are good at painting and are the best horse rider I've ever known."

Ms. Martinez interrupted. "Girls, it's time to head to the cafeteria."

What about me? Tess thought as Erin gathered her things for lunch. *Do I balance out?*

❋

"Thank you for helping, girls. I have a special privilege for you today. One of our serving ladies is sick; so you'll be helping hand the food to the students." Mrs. Steadman gave Erin and Tess each a plastic package. "I'll be back in a few minutes to set you up." With that she turned and went to the back kitchen.

Erin opened her package first and pulled out an elastic-banded hair net. "Special privilege? Is she joking? No way am I wearing this net over my head!" Erin said, giggling. She stretched the net over her face. "Look, I'm Spider Man."

"I didn't think we were going to serve food. The last helpers just prepared the tacos in the back," Tess said. "How embarrassing!" She wound her hair around the back and pulled the net over her ears. "You can't see my ears can you?"

"Nope. Well, I suppose we'd better make the best of it." Erin turned as Mrs. Steadman came back and directed the girls to stand in front of the mini-pizza pans.

"You just place the spatula under a pizza if someone

chooses it for his entrée and slide the pizza onto the plate. I'll be working right behind you and will replace the pans as you run out of product."

"Okay," Tess said.

The first few classes weren't too bad. The first and second graders stared in wide-eyed wonder at two students serving pizza, but when Tess saw who was scheduled for the second lunch period, she nudged Erin. "Look who's coming."

"I say, the old girl is a cafeteria lady now," Tyler boomed out, not embarrassed at all to be heard throughout the lunchroom.

"What a lovely 'do," Big Al mocked, nodding toward her hair net.

"Do you want pizza?" Tess said grumpily. This definitely had not been in her plan.

"As long as you don't touch it," Big Al said. Tess slid her spatula under a pizza. She would have touched it, just to bug him, but she didn't want him to holler and get Mrs. Steadman on her case.

"How about you, young man?" she asked her brother.

"No thanks. I'll take a sandwich. Safer," Tyler answered. "Ta ta. See you after work." He and Big Al cleared the line and went to sit down.

Tess and Erin had a few minutes before the third lunch period, so they rested. Tess's ankle hurt from standing on it. That was not a hopeful sign for tryouts Saturday. But she knew it wouldn't help to complain.

"You forgot to tell me what your big surprise was," Tess reminded Erin.

"Oh yeah." Erin grew pink. "Well, I'm wearing something else new—besides the hair net, that is."

"Really?" Tess guessed what it was by her friend's pleased blush. "Did your mom take you shopping?"

"Yep. Yesterday."

"Well, now we're matching sisters again," Tess said. "Let's promise to do all important things together."

"Okay," Erin agreed. Then, swapping their identical charm bracelets, they sealed the deal.

"Girls," Mrs. Steadman called, "back to work."

Tess lumbered to her feet, tentatively putting her weight on her bad ankle. "I never realized how hard it would be to stand for a couple of hours!"

"If you think that's bad, look who's heading up the line." Erin positioned herself behind the counter as they both caught sight of the Coronado Club, the ones who had tortured Tess about her ears last September.

"Oh, great," Tess said.

"My, my, my," Lauren remarked, pushing her shiny hair behind her ears as she approached the counter. "Can you tell us what you're serving today, girls?" Behind her Melody let out a high-pitched giggle. It really annoyed Tess.

"Lasagna," Tess said. "What does it look like?"

"Well, it looks like pizza to me. But maybe this is what lasagna looks like at your house," Lauren said, twisting a real gold ring on her finger. "You two look positively dreamy in those hair nets. I think I saw them in Geek Weekly."

"I wouldn't know; I don't read it," Erin said. Tess elbowed her under the counter.

"Would you like a piece of pizza?" Tess asked sweetly.

"No thanks." Lauren looked back at Melody and Colleen. Andrea trailed all three. "Let's have something safer." She picked up a sandwich, and the others followed suit. "Have a good time, girls." She turned back to Colleen and Melody. Andrea tagged along. "We'll limit our work in the cafeteria to the mural art when we make the team next month. Let the unartistic serve the food."

"Ooh, she drives me crazy!" Erin said. "I guess that means they're going to try out for the mural team. I hope not. They always win everything, and I want to be on the team!"

"Yeah, well they'll have to fight us for it, won't they?" Tess said. She added, "But the worst part is, she's so smooth and pretty I really do feel like I should be in Geek Weekly when I'm next to her."

"Me, too," Erin admitted. "It's like, I feel pretty good about myself most of the time. But then I compare myself to someone like her, and I don't look so good anymore."

"That's just how I feel." Tess served another mini-pizza. "But it's not like I'd want her personality. Maybe just her hair."

Erin nodded her agreement and then turned to signal Mrs. Steadman that the pizza tray was empty.

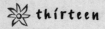

thirteen

Exit Sign

Friday Night, January 24

The movie theater wasn't dark yet, but Tess's eyes still had to adjust in time to chase after her brother. "I want to sit in the middle," Tess said as she ran down the long, dimly lit movie theater aisle before Tyler could choose his front-row favorite. She ignored her ankle, which protested the quick moves.

"Why? It's so much better in the front," Tyler said. "Close up, where all the action is."

"'Cause I can't see anything up there." Tess turned sideways and inched her way into a center aisle. She chose one seat and then jumped up and moved on as she noticed a lady with a smokestack hairdo sitting in front of her. Passing by a seat next to a man with a hacking cough, she finally found one. "Is this okay?"

"I guess." Tyler lifted up his shoe. A long, thick string of dirty gum bound his sole to the floor. "I say, a herd of swine has been in this theater." He rubbed his shoe against the floor, and eventually the gum broke free.

"Could you please decide on a seat?" their father asked.

"I'm balancing this feeding-trough-sized popcorn, and it's about to spill. Not to mention Tyler's gummy spiders." Tess rolled her eyes. Dad always wanted things orderly.

Tess winced as her mother's gently protruding tummy almost bumped into the bald head of a man seated in the row just ahead of them. "Okay," her mom said, approving the seat choice. "Sit down."

Tess flipped down her chair and sat. Tyler flipped his up and down a few times and finally took a seat himself. Molly Thomas edged in next to him, and her dad settled into the seat on the end. They munched popcorn in relative silence while the premovie advertisements flashed across the screen.

"Have you seen me?" lit up the screen, and several unsavory men's mug-shot frowns glared from the screen.

"Hey, Tess, some of your friends are in the movies." Tyler laughed, pointing to them.

"My friends? News flash! Your friends are more likely to be up there. Like Big Al."

"Did Tess tell you guys about her day as a cafeteria lady?" Tyler elbowed his sister.

"No, tell us about it," her mother said.

"There's not much to tell. We served pizza and worked all four lunch periods."

"I'll bet that was fun," her mother said.

"Yeah, but she wouldn't even give me an extra dessert," Tyler teased.

Tess tossed a popcorn kernel at him. "I might have if you had asked me."

"Last time we were sitting in an auditorium, it was for Tyler's performance." Mrs. Thomas leaned over and kissed Tyler's cheek. "I was so proud. Still am."

Tyler blushed, scanning the room nervously to see if any of his friends had witnessed the smooch. "Yeah, well…" He fidgeted a bit, then asked, "Dad, will you take me to play some of the video games in the lobby? The movie doesn't start for fifteen more minutes, and I'm bored."

His dad shook the popcorn container. "Sure, and I'll get some more munchies. There must be a hole in the bottom of this popcorn. It's almost gone."

"Yeah, yeah," Tess's mother said. "We'll hold the seats while you're gone."

Once they left, Tess scooted over toward her mother. "Can you believe it's only been one week since my party? So much has happened."

"How was practice today?" her mother asked. "Are you ready for tryouts tomorrow?"

"I think so," Tess said even though her stomach leaped at the thought. "I did really well on the bars, but I need a little work on the beam and mats. Stefani hasn't let me work on either one since I hurt my ankle, but I need to show her what I can do tomorrow. She looked at it today and said I can try. I think I'm as good as the others on the vault, just a little out of practice. I hope my ankle is well by morning."

"It seems to be healing quickly. But don't push yourself. How is Erin? I haven't heard you say much about her this week." Mrs. Thomas popped a Junior Mint into her mouth. "Baby likes candy," she joked. "I can't wait to see what the baby is like when he or she is born. Maybe he or she will be a musician like Tyler."

Or a nothing like me, Tess thought. She didn't want her mother to know what she was thinking though, so she said, "Erin's great. She wants me to come over to her grandparents' house next week. They're getting a new mare. And she gets to name her!"

"Oh fun, Tess. But will you have time? I mean, isn't gymnastics every day?"

"Yeah. I thought maybe I could take a day off. You know."

"I don't think the coach is going to let you do that as soon as you make the team. Not if you're serious."

Tess pushed her box of Lemon Heads back into her purse. "That reminds me. I'd better not eat any more. Fat." Tess tapped her tummy. "Oh hey, Mom, I copied something down for you last night. Dad told me about the aminopolicas."

"The what?" her mother asked.

"You know, the test to see if the baby is okay."

"Amniocentesis," her mother corrected with a smile.

"Yeah. Well, when I was looking on my day-to-day calendar, I found a Bible verse that I thought was just right." Tess unfolded the piece of paper she had stuffed into her pocket and read, "'You made my whole being. You formed me in my mother's body. I praise you because you made me in an amazing and wonderful way. What you have done is wonderful. I know this very well.' Psalm 139:13 and 14."

"That's very nice, Tess." Her mother reached an arm around to hug her. "I didn't know the Bible had things like that in it."

"It does. And other stuff. I haven't read it all yet. But it's all truth. I was thinking, even if the baby does have something wrong, it would be okay. Maybe he or she would be really sweet, like Heidi."

"You're right, Tess. I hope the baby is well, but we'll love this baby no matter what he or she is like, just like we do you and Tyler. It's great you're thinking a lot about God making this baby just right. But maybe you should be thinking about how he made you just right. Are you thinking you need to be a superstar at gymnastics to be special?"

"No," Tess said, wiping her buttery hands on a recycled brown napkin. But she knew her mother had hit home. "That's not the same."

"Why not? God didn't make any mistakes with you."

"No, I guess not." Pretending to focus on the ads flashing across the screen, she considered her mother's words. Did Tess praise God for the way he had made her? Did she believe what he had done with her was wonderful? Did she know it very well, like the verse said?

A wave of sickness rolled through Tess's stomach, and not from too many Lemon Heads. What about riding? What about Erin? Would their friendship wither when gymnastics took over her life? Would she and her dad have to drop out of the Grand Canyon Rim-to-Rim? She stared at the screen, recalling Stefani's voice today—"You're getting much better, Tess. Keep it up"—and remembering the warm flush of pride at hearing those hard-won words. A bright neon-green exit sign caught her eye. She took it as an indication it was a good time to exit this conversation.

"I think the movie is about to start," she said. "I'll get the guys." Standing up, she turned sideways and inched her way out of the row again, then strode up the aisle as if her ankle didn't hurt. Little pearls of light reflected on the maroon carpet, guiding her way. It reminded her of last month's memory verse from Sunday school.

"Your word is a lamp to my feet and a light for my path," Tess whispered to herself.

fourteen

Tryouts

Saturday, January 25

"Glad to see you showed up early," Joann confided as she changed alongside Tess. "It'll give you a chance to work through your routine before officially trying out." Slipping into a shimmering gold leotard that beautifully contrasted with her mahogany skin, Joann looked cool and poised.

"Thanks." Tess felt tacky in her shorts and T-shirt. "I'm feeling pretty good about it. If I can just count on my ankle not to act up."

"That was a piece of bad luck," Joann agreed. "It'll make things much tougher."

Thanks, Tess thought. *Just what I need to hear.* She smoothed down her shirt and pulled up her socks. Once again, she twisted her hair into a loose, knotted ponytail.

Joann teased, "Nice ears."

"Are they that obvious?" Tess asked, clapping her hands over them.

"No no, I'm only joking. Nobody else notices them." Joann slammed shut her locker. "Ready?"

"Yes." They walked out into the gym.

"I'm going over to the mats. I'll talk to you after tryouts. Good luck!" Joann waved, and Tess waved back. She went over to the beam first since it was the most difficult.

After mounting the beam, she walked surefootedly—just like a goat, she thought to herself. Her ankle seemed strong—so far. But would it hold up?

After warming up a bit she did a perfect cartwheel and didn't fall off. Heady with achievement, she did a round-off onto the mat and held her arms up in triumph. Stefani was right, she had improved! With confidence now, Tess moved on to practice her floor exercise moves and a couple of back handsprings. It seemed like only a few minutes before she heard the coaches page them to their stations.

Her ankle started to throb, but just a little. She rubbed at the skin under the bandage and hoped it would give her just another hour. That's all she asked.

Lots of girls were warming up at different stations, all trying out on various equipment. Parents cheered from the stands, and a couple of portable stereos provided the music for the floor exercise.

"Level-eight tryouts will begin on the bars, level-seven tryouts on the vault, level-six tryouts on the beam, and level-five on the mats. Please report to the appropriate station." Tess shrugged her shoulders, a little nervous now, and caught her mother's wave out of the corner of her eye. She waved back, trying to ignore the trickle of sweat coursing down her spine.

Soon it was her turn to work. She ran from the corner of the navy-blue mat and did a cartwheel, back handspring, and a flip. Then, after a little improvised dancing, she did a few more moves, only messing up one time with her flip. Her mom held up her thumb, and Tess glanced at Stefani, who smiled. There. That wasn't too bad, was it?

Watching the other competitors, Tess noticed that lots of them were younger than she, maybe third or fourth grade. And they were good. Nobody messed up any more than Tess had, and one or two of them made a perfect attempt on one of the allotted two tries. Tess decided she was better than about half and worse than about half. She stopped herself. *Quit comparing yourself to others*, she thought.

"Good job, girls. Nice showing. Let's move over to the balance beam," Stefani directed the level-five participants. Nervous prickles stung the inside of Tess's stomach, and a wave of nausea crested within. *Please, God*, she silently prayed, *don't let me barf. Let me do a good job.*

The perfect little girl she had noticed on the bars the other day mounted the beam first. Tess felt a little better when she saw the girl take a minor misstep. Then Tess flushed, not wanting to be pleased at someone else's mistakes, but realizing she was, a little.

"Tess Thomas, you're next." Stefani motioned her onto the beam. Tess mounted, her knees weaker than they had ever been. Her ankle was getting warm now, and the throbbing was more noticeable. She could feel it swelling up. Carefully she stepped and then dipped her foot below the beam level. *No mistakes yet. Concentrate. Don't look around you.* A piece of sweaty hair slipped out of the knot and slid down the side of her cheek as she concentrated. *Come on. Back to the end of the beam and then cartwheel.*

And then, in what seemed like slow motion, she sensed her ankle give way and her foot slip off the board, pulling her body right along with it. A nanosecond later she was on her bottom, on the mat. Face bright red, she looked up at the crowd around her.

"It's okay, Tess. Take another try. You're allowed two, you know," the assistant coach encouraged her.

She mounted again. While her ankle felt hot, the throbbing wasn't any worse. This time she looked at her mother, who gave her the "I love you" sign with her thumb, pointer finger, and pinkie. *I will not cry,* Tess willed. First stepping and dipping, she made a perfect cartwheel.

She went for the round-off. She fell again. Her spirits and hopes crashed to the mat with her. *I'm sorry if I embarrassed you, Lord,* she said inside, wiping away a tear and pulling herself together for the bars. That dumb ankle! It was all her dad's fault for making her go hiking. She had told him she was tired.

After tryouts she met Joann in the locker room.

"How'd it go?" Joann asked her. "I saw your mat routine, and it looked really good. You have a lot of skill. You could be really good if you worked at it."

"Thanks," Tess mumbled. "I biffed it on the beam though. I fell twice." She stuffed the sweaty T-shirt into her backpack and shook baby powder over her arms. "How did you do?"

"Well…," Joann started, and Tess could see her struggle.

"You did a perfect job, right?" Tess asked dejectedly.

"I don't think I made too many mistakes," Joann agreed. "But don't forget, I practice almost every day. You dropped out for a year and a half. And your ankle is bad."

"I know," Tess muttered. "And I'm sure you never biffed anything." Tess was surprised at the venom in her voice. She softened. "I'd better hurry up. I think my mom is waiting for me."

"Oh." Joann turned her back to Tess before saying, "I wish my mom would come sometime."

"Doesn't she ever watch you perform?"

"No. She's a diplomat. She moves around a lot. It's one reason I stayed with my dad when they divorced."

"Oh."

Joann's back was still turned so Tess couldn't see her face. She had the feeling that if she could, she would see tears.

"Yeah, well." Tess closed her locker, not knowing what else to say.

"Anyway," Joann straightened up and closed her own locker, "they'll give you a call tonight and let you know if you made the team. Then they don't answer the phone until Monday."

"Okay. Good luck." Tess swung her bag over her shoulder.

"You, too," Joann said, walking out to wait for her dad.

"You did a great job, honey. How's your ankle?" Mom said as she ground the Jeep's gears, and the car took off. "Wow! When did they put that tree in?" She swerved, just barely missing an ornamental pine on the way out.

"It's been there all week, Mom." Tess hoped Stefani wasn't looking. Or Joann. Or anybody, for that matter. "The ankle's okay. I rewrapped it. I don't know how you can say I did a good job. I fell off the beam twice."

"Yes, you did. But you also had a great floor routine, and you did just fine on the bars and the vault."

Tess stared out the window, trying to concentrate on the

masses of gaudy purple bougainvillea flowers climbing the telephone poles and arching over the entrance to the drugstore they had just passed.

"These things happen. Your job now is to focus on having done a great job overall. When will they let you know?"

"They'll call me tonight." She waved as their car passed Joann's car on the street. *Why bother?* she thought. *Stefani could have just told me I didn't make it before I left.*

"Joann did a good job," Tess's mother noted.

"Yeah. She felt really bad 'cause her parents are divorced and her mom never comes to her meets."

"Well, I guess her life isn't so perfect after all." Mrs. Thomas kept her eyes on the road. "That's the trouble with comparing yourself to others. You never know the whole story."

Tess nodded, her mind replaying her performance over and over. If only she hadn't fallen.

fifteen

Don't Look Now

Saturday Afternoon, January 25

Less than a minute after Tess tumbled onto her bed, a sharp rap on the door interrupted her rest.

"Tess, don't forget we're hiking in fifteen minutes," her father called in, and she heard him walk away from the door.

Great. She was tired! She had already spent the morning working out, and she wanted to read awhile. Plus, what if the coaches called while she was gone? Pushing herself off the bed, she went to ask her dad if they could skip the hike this once.

As she approached her parents' bedroom door, she could hear her mom and dad arguing. "She's had a busy morning, Jim, and I think she should stay home to rest her ankle. I don't know if she's done her homework yet, and I'm sure she's planning to go to church tomorrow."

"You know, I'm trying to teach these children some responsibility," her dad said back, his voice rising. Tess knew she shouldn't eavesdrop, but she was paralyzed by the conversation. "She made the commitment to hike, to do the Rim-to-Rim, and to train for it. She has to learn to keep her word. Maybe she'll have to drop out of church for a while. Yeah, I think that might be a good idea."

"All I'm saying is you can be inflexible," Mrs. Thomas answered, her voice tired. "We can talk about it with her later."

"We'll take a short hike, just to Squaw Peak. But she needs to respect the promise she made about training." Tess heard her father open his closet door, probably to get his hiking boots, and she scooted back to her room.

Slowly pulling on her own boots, she thought about what she had overheard. It was true she had promised to hike, and she liked it. But she was really tired today. Didn't Dad ever get tired? Yanking on her second boot, she pulled the laces tight with frustration. Then she stomped into the garage to wait for her father.

"I say, old bean, aren't you the sporty one?" Tyler sat on the floor surrounded by scrap wood and leftover mesh from the screen door.

"What's that supposed to mean?"

"My, my, don't be so touchy. I was simply observing the vast amount of time you spend in athletic pursuit these days. First gymnastics, now hiking." Tyler nodded toward her boots.

"Not by choice," Tess muttered. "What are you doing?"

"Building a bug trap. So I can catch more of Hercules' meals and not spend so much money at the pet store on second-rate crickets."

"What's the difference between a first- and a second-rate cricket?" Tess asked him.

"Well, old bean, a first-rate cricket has a large, soft body. I can sometimes catch them outside. Second-rate crickets are smaller and cost more. Hercules likes the first-rate ones, and I can save some allowance money if I catch them."

"Sicko," Tess said but smiled at her brother's creativity. He did have a good mind to think of this bug trap.

"Ready?" Her father shut the door from the house to the garage.

"I guess so." Tess stifled a yawn and climbed into the Jeep. She stared through the open window at the landscape as they drove through the residential streets and up into the park where Squaw Peak sat. A brisk wind scoured the treeless landscape, picking up grains of sandstone and stinging her eyes. She zipped her windbreaker to her neck and exited the car when Dad parked it.

"Ouch!" Tess stumbled over a clump of Desert Spoon wilting at the trailhead.

"Did you hurt your ankle?" her dad asked.

"No." Tess wanted her ankle to hurt so she could go home, but it seemed to be okay.

"Well, pick up your feet," admonished her father.

"I am," Tess wailed.

"Then pick your eyes up, too." Dad forged ahead. Silently, Tess trudged behind him.

She normally would have been glad to notice the tiny bug families nesting in holes pecked into the cacti surrounding her, or the few wildflower blossoms willing to sprout in January. Today she marched by them barely casting a lazy eye in their direction. Only the sound of voices coming down the mountain as she and her dad tramped up motivated her to look past her father's footsteps.

Could it be? Tess snapped out of her daze.

It was.

Tom, Erin's brother, and Mr. Janssen were walking down the mountain as Tess and her father were walking up. Quickly, Tess tucked her shirt under her jacket; it had sloppily slipped out. Spreading her fingers, she smoothed her wind-worn hair into place and wiped the sweat from her forehead. One last thing: She gently pinched each of her cheeks with her right thumb and forefinger. One of her mother's old movies said it brought out a natural blush.

Her dad slowed down. "Isn't that Erin's father?"

"Yes." Tess tried to look both calm and surprised at the same time.

"Hello there!" Mr. Janssen called down to them. Tess and her father waved back but didn't call out in return, choosing to wait until the parties met.

"How are you two today?" Mr. Janssen asked Tess.

"Fine, just fine." Tess answered.

Tom smiled at her, his dimpled cheeks pink from exertion, but his blond hair as perfect as ever. "I thought Erin said you were at gymnastics tryouts today," he said. "But maybe not, since I see you're wearing a bandage." He motioned to her wrapped ankle.

"Oh, that." Tess shrugged, trying to look cool and un-affected. "I still tried out. It's healing." But inside she was thinking, *Wow! He remembered something about me!*

"Yeah, my dad and I are going to hike across the Grand Canyon in May; so we're out here training."

"That sounds great," Tom said. "I never knew anyone who would be willing to hike across the entire Grand Canyon."

"Just South Rim to North Rim," Tess hastily explained.

Tom smiled, and Tess read real admiration in his eyes. "Still, that's great. My sister always said you were a little different, and I guess she was right."

Tess's father and Mr. Janssen made small talk for another minute before saying good-bye.

"Well, good luck on the hiking," Tom called out to her.

Tess waved. Suddenly energized, she picked up both her feet and the pace.

"Look at those swollen cacti!" she pointed out to her father. "They must still be holding a lot of water." She chattered on for a minute or two, then looked up at her dad, who smiled at her.

"You suddenly have a lot of energy," he commented.

Tess figured he probably knew why, but she wasn't about to talk with him about that. "Let's just finish so I can get back to hear if the coaches called," she said, charging ahead.

❋

"We're back! Did anyone call?" Tess burst into the kitchen.

"Yes." Her mother stood over a steaming kettle and broke handfuls of straw-like spaghetti noodles before dropping them in. "Stefani. She said you could call her back when you got in."

"Great. Thanks!" Tess kicked off her hiking shoes and ran to her room. Hands shaking, she dialed the number on the back of the gym's brochure.

"Hello, may I speak with Stefani please?"

"This is she," came the voice across the line.

"This is Tess Thomas, calling you back. Did I make it?" she burst out.

Stefani laughed. "Well, Tess, you did."

"All right!" Tess almost dropped the phone in joy.

"Hold on there, kiddo," Stefani continued. "I have a couple of conditions."

"Sure. Yes, anything," Tess said.

"You have a lot of potential, even though you're sort of rusty since you skipped a little more than a year. So I'll need you to commit to being at every practice, no excuses."

"No problem! I'll do it," Tess rushed on without stopping to think.

"Well, maybe you had better talk to your parents about it first. And one more thing, Tess."

"Yes?"

"I'd like you to think about why gymnastics is so important to you. Like I said, you have a lot of skill, but I didn't see a love for the sport, a desire to improve because you wanted to be better. I know you are new, so maybe it's there, and I just didn't see it. But it's something to consider because you'll need to love the sport if you're going to practice five days a week."

"Okay. Thanks, Stefani."

"You can come in to pay your additional gym fees Monday afternoon."

"Thanks!" Tess said. "See you later."

"'Bye." Stefani hung up the phone.

All right!

The phone hadn't rested for a minute when it rang again. Tess hoped it wasn't Stefani changing her mind.

"Hello?"

"Hi! It's me, Erin. How did tryouts go?"

"I made it!" Tess shouted into the phone.

"Good job!" Erin said. "I knew you could do it! Let's celebrate next week! I asked my mom about Tuesday. You can come home from school with me, and my mom will drive us over to ride the horses. You can eat here, too. Oh, Tess," she continued, "I'm so glad your practices are over! I've really missed being together."

"Um, yeah. Me, too," Tess said. "I'd better go. I haven't told my parents yet. I'll see you tomorrow morning, right?"

"Yep. See ya later!" Erin clicked off, and Tess hung up the phone.

What about Tuesday? Stefani said Tess couldn't miss even one practice, which meant she couldn't go home with Erin Tuesday. Or any day. She stared at herself in the mirror, and reality struck home. Five days a week. What had she gotten herself into? She pushed the thought away.

"I made it!" she sang into the kitchen.

"Oh, wonderful, honey!" Her mother gave her a hug. Mr. Thomas came in and gave her a high-five.

"She said I need to make sure the fees are all right with you guys and also that it's okay that I make it to practice five days a week."

"Sure, if that's what you want." Her father sat down. "But to do that, Tess, something will have to go. I know I've pushed the hiking, but I can cancel it, if you want. Or maybe you need to drop church for a little while. You can't do everything. But you can do what matters most." She looked at him and knew he thought that gymnastics mattered most.

Tess wasn't as sure.

But she could picture her mom and dad sitting in the bleachers clapping as she won trophies at the meets, their eyes sparkling like they did when Tyler performed. Or her mom snapping pictures of Tess on the bars, and Mom smiling that special smile she had when she was thinking of the baby. It would make it all worthwhile, Tess convinced herself. It really would.

Later that evening she sat down to finish her Sunday school homework. "Choose one of the following verses," she read. "Look it up. Copy it in your notebook. What does it mean for you?"

Choosing one at random, Tess used her pencil eraser to push through her Bible to Psalm 34:4-5. She copied, "I asked the Lord for help, and he answered me. He saved me from all that I feared. Those who go to him for help are happy. They are never disgraced."

Closing her eyes, she drank in the sound of a cricket not yet in Tyler's grasp as it scratched its squeaky fiddle outside her window. "Jesus," she prayed, "what should I do about gymnastics? I'm so happy I made it because that means I'm good enough. But maybe Stefani is right. And Dad wants me to choose between gymnastics, church, and hiking. Whatever I choose I'll disappoint someone, maybe lots of people. But I really want to be good and have Grandma and Grandpa Thomas talk about me to cousin Jane for a change. I'm doing like that verse said, God. I'm asking you for help. Please tell me what to do." She listened intently in prayer. But nothing came.

sixteen

Love Lists

Sunday, January 26

"Did you ask your mother about Tuesday?" Erin said as she and Tess poured themselves some punch before Sunday school started.

"No, I didn't." An uneasy pang jolted Tess. "I have to figure it out, about gymnastics and all that. I'll talk with her tonight though, I promise. Then I'll call you." Popping a cinnamon sugar donut hole into her mouth, she led the way toward the chairs she and Erin usually sat in.

"Do you guys mind if I sit with you today?" Melissa plopped herself down on the seat on the other side of Tess.

"Not at all," Erin said.

"Thanks. Tess, are you still planning to work in the nursery?" Tess and Melissa worked together in the toddler nursery once a month. Melissa's mother was in charge.

"Yes, I am. Did I tell you that Mrs. Fye called me a couple of weeks ago to see if I could baby-sit?"

"Actually, I did know." Melissa leaned closer. "She called my mother and said her daughter always babbled about you after you worked in the nursery and could she have your number. I'm glad she called."

"I never guessed that working in the nursery would lead to that! And the pay is good, too," Tess said.

Sjana, one of the teachers, motioned for them all to stand up as she turned on the CD player to some worship music. Erin winked at Tess, who smiled back.

"I like the singing part best," Tess said.

"I know," Erin answered.

Fifteen minutes later they sat down to work on their lesson. Sjana started. "Hey guys, settle down. Does anyone want to share what he or she did with last week's lesson?"

"I looked up 1 Timothy 4:8," one boy volunteered. "It made me think about how much time I spend on sports compared to how much time I spend reading the Bible or helping others." Tess wanted to look up the verse right then, but it might seem rude to the next person who talked. She penciled in the verse on the inside flap of her Bible so she would remember to look it up later.

"Anyone else?" Sjana said. A couple of others shared their verses and what the scripture had meant to them. Tess raised her hand to share about Psalm 139:13-14, even though it wasn't one of the suggested verses. Time ran out before Sjana could call on her, though.

"We have a fun group-exercise for you this week," Adam, the other teacher, spoke up. "They're called 'love lists.'" Tess turned to look at Erin, who raised her eyebrows. Sometimes what Adam and Sjana thought was fun was not so fun for the class.

"I felt really convinced this week that we need to spend more of our time here encouraging one another," Adam said. "I was reading Hebrews chapter 10 for my own Bible study, and I came across verse 25. It says we should meet together at church and encourage one another. Let's break up into groups of about, ah, eight, I guess. Here's a piece of paper. Each of you write your name at the top."

Sjana came around the room handing out pieces of paper and stubby pencils with no erasers.

"Then I want you to sit in your circles and pass the papers around," Adam continued. "On each person's paper I want you to write something to encourage that person. It might be something you noticed that he or she does well, or a verse that comes to mind, or anything you appreciate about that person. Then we'll meet together as a group again in about fifteen minutes."

After Adam finished talking, Tess and Erin scooted their chairs so they could make a small circle with Melissa and four or five others.

Nobody said anything for a minute. So Melissa jumped in. "I guess we should just pass our papers to the right, and then write something on each paper. Keep circling them until we're all done." She thrust her paper toward Tess, and Tess handed hers to Erin. Erin handed hers to a girl they hardly knew sitting to her right.

Tess scribbled, "Melissa, thank you for inviting me to work in the nursery. I really like it, and it makes me feel so much more like I belong at this church. You are a good friend." Then she handed the paper to Erin, and so it went for a few minutes until they had all written something on each paper.

"Let's get back together now, people. Finish up," Adam called out. Brushing some powdered sugar from her shirt,

Tess scooted her chair around. The group finished the time talking about encouraging each other.

"I told my family you made the gymnastics squad," Erin said on the way out to her car.

"Oh. What did they say?"

"They thought it was great, of course." Erin leaned against the Suburban as they waited for her parents and brothers.

"Hi, guys. Pay me a dollar, and I'll let you into the car," Tom teased.

Tess looked up. He had such a good sense of humor.

"Ha ha. Pay me a dollar, and I'll let you sit next to me," Erin shot back. She rolled her eyes at Tess, who, of course, smiled back.

Tom opened the car door, and soon Erin's parents arrived, too, and they were on their way home.

"What did you do in Sunday school today?" Mrs. Janssen asked.

"Nothing," Josh answered. Josh Janssen was the same age as Tyler, and it showed.

"Nothing at all? You all sat in silence the entire time?" Mr. Janssen teased. "How about you, girls?" he asked. Tess liked how he always included her, as if she were one of the family.

"We wrote lists about what we liked about each other. It was sort of strange, but fun, too," Erin answered.

"I guess yours is blank, huh?" Tom said.

"That wasn't very nice," Erin's dad said. "Maybe it would be good for you to say something nice about Erin, and Tess, too."

Tess flushed from neck to hairline. This was one time

when it would have been okay for Mr. Janssen not to include her.

"Uh, okay," Tom said. He looked as if he had swallowed a live fish.

"Erin, you, um, you ride horses really well. And you are kind, I guess," Tom said. He looked at Tess. Suddenly she was really glad that Erin had told him Tess had made the team so he had something good he could say about her.

"Tess, you are a good hiker." He hesitated. "I think it's cool that you're not like the other girls because you're willing to be different, like hiking the Rim-to-Rim." He turned away from the girls, and Tess saw pink tinge his ears with discomfort.

Hiking! she thought. She had never considered hiking as being cool, something that set her apart. But she guessed it was—and she loved it, too. So, apparently, did Tom.

✻

"The doctor called this morning!" her mother sang out a few minutes later as Tess set her Bible down on the kitchen table and went to make herself a sandwich.

"On Sunday? With good news?" Tess asked eagerly.

"Yes. They work Sundays at that clinic. And the baby seems just fine," her mother said.

"And…is it a boy or a girl?" Tess asked.

"We told them we didn't want to know." Her mother smiled, handing Tess the jar of peanut butter.

"Are you kidding? I want to know!"

"Well, you'll just have to wait like the rest of us," her mother said. "It's fun to have a surprise." She busied herself wiping the counter. "Could you please pick the grapefruit after lunch? The trees are bowing low to the ground, and the fruit is going to drop off if we don't get to it soon."

"Sure," Tess agreed.

After polishing off her sandwich, she headed outside. Taking deep breaths of the sweetly spiced air, she wondered again at the miracle of trees producing fruit while so much of the country was up to its hat rack in snow. Her mother had taught Tess that if she waited until the first real cold snap before picking the fruit, the cold would give them an extra shot of sugar, which made them even sweeter. As she rested each piece of fruit in her palm, she twisted it slowly until it snapped right off the tree. After she had picked about ten grapefruits, she sat down and peeled one for her dessert.

"Oh, yeah," she said to herself, "the list from church." After popping a sweet-and-sour section of grapefruit into her mouth, she reached into her pocket and pulled out the list.

She read aloud, "Tess, you are so good with kids. You make a good baby-sitter and will be a good mom someday. Your new little brother or sister will be lucky to have you." *Must have been Melissa*, she thought.

"You are always brave and raise your hand and don't look stupid if you don't get called on," someone else wrote. Wow, she hadn't thought of herself as brave.

"You are the best friend anyone could ever ask for. You always listen to me and are loyal no matter what." Erin. Tess smiled. Her Secret Sister was the best friend she could ever ask for, too. She would remember to send Erin a secret letter tomorrow. Oh yeah, Tess had to ask her mother about the girls' riding horses this week.

Sitting against the gnarled trunk of the grapefruit tree, Tess remembered what Tom had said about hiking. It was true, she guessed; not many girls did hike the Rim-to-Rim—not that she had ever heard of anyway. Staring up at the glossy green leaves, she asked the Lord, "What should I do about gymnastics on Tuesday?" Usually she struggled to understand what the Lord told her, so the swift answer surprised her. It also bothered her, because she knew people would be disappointed.

✳ seventeen

Decisions

Monday Afternoon, January 27

"So, first we're going to the gym, and then we're going to the mall, right?" Erin asked as she and Tess walked in front of Coronado Elementary School to meet Tess's mother. A cool breeze blew over the mountains and clipped their shoulders where they stood.

"Right. And I have a surprise for you at the mall. It will astound you!"

"Ooh, I love surprises! Give me a hint."

"Can't cut you a break here, sis. It'll only take me a few minutes at the gym; then we can go shopping. Did you bring your money?"

"Yep." Erin pulled her wallet out of her backpack to show Tess. "I hope you'll help me pick out some new jeans. You have such good taste."

"Of course I will. I always think the same about you! And I brought the coupons you signed me up for. So we can go to the Christian bookstore to buy a book or a CD and also split some ice cream."

"Yum, that sounds good. Are you eating ice cream again?"

"Yes." Tess pointed. "There's my mom."

The chrome-trimmed Jeep pulled up in front of the school, narrowly missing a prickly pear cactus cowering at the driveway entrance. Molly Thomas drove over the curb and abruptly halted the vehicle.

"Hi, girls. Ready?" she called, leaning over to open the door for Tess.

"Yep. Are we waiting for Tyler?" Tess asked, scanning the emptying schoolyard for her brother.

"No, he's going home with Big Al again today. They're working on a science project."

"He spends a lot of time with Big Alien these days," Tess commented.

"He has other friends, too," her mother said. "All buckled in?" The girls nodded. "Let's go!" She pulled out of the driveway and headed toward the gym.

As the car traveled down the side streets, Tess nervously counted palm trees to pass the minutes until they arrived. Baby royal palms squatted on fat round trunks that looked like two-feet-tall pineapples. Green tufted leaves sprouted from their tops. Sturdy date palms rested on thick-scaled pillars, stretching their fruit-jeweled crowns a hundred feet into the air. She had counted fifty trees before her mother pulled the Jeep into the gym's parking lot.

"You're awfully quiet, " Erin whispered. "Are you feeling okay?"

"Yes." Tess grabbed her backpack.

"I'm going to run to the post office while you do this. I need to mail some ad copy today." Her mother waved a thick envelope. "Maybe Erin can sit on the bench while you talk with Stefani. I'll be back in about fifteen minutes." The girls exited the car, and Molly Thomas drove away.

"Do you mind waiting here? I'll be out in just a minute," Tess said.

"Okay." Erin plopped down on a wooden bench just outside the gym's entrance and pulled a book out of her backpack. "I'll be right here."

Tess gritted her teeth and went into the gym. "May I talk with Stefani, please?" she asked the receptionist.

"Are you leaving a payment? If so, I can take it. Do you have your signed forms?" The receptionist slid the glass window across metal runners and held out her hand, anticipating a check and some papers.

"No, uh, I need to talk with Stefani," Tess answered.

"All right." The receptionist paged the coach, and a couple of seconds later Stefani came out.

"Hi, Tess. Come on back." She ushered Tess into a tiny, trophy-filled office and motioned for her to take a seat. "What can I do for you?"

"Well," Tess perched on the edge of her chair. "I've been thinking about what you said. You know about not missing any practices and did I really love gymnastics. I think the answer," she gulped, "is no."

"I see," Stefani sat back in her chair. Tess saw the coach's face flush and her jaw set like Tess's dad's did when he was angry. Stefani waited for Tess to continue.

"You know, when Joann talked about gymnastics, it reminded me that I used to be good. And it seemed like all my friends were good at something, and I couldn't think of what I was good at."

Stefani nodded brusquely.

"So I thought maybe I'd go back to gymnastics," Tess said. "But when I thought about all the things I'd have to give up to do it, I decided it really wasn't what I wanted."

"Well, Tess, I wish you had decided this before the others were cut. Someone was cut from the team that really, really wanted it. Don't you feel a little selfish?"

Man, she hadn't thought Stefani would be this mad. "I'm sorry," Tess swallowed. "I hope you can call someone back."

"I can," Stefani said. "You know the deposit was non-refundable."

"Oh." Now she would have to tell Mom and Dad that she couldn't get the money back either.

Stefani continued. "But it's better to find out now before you waste your time and mine and while we can let someone else have your place on the team. It would be a shame to waste your athletic ability though. Are you planning to be involved with another sport?"

"I hike a lot with my dad. So I guess that's my sport for now. We're going to hike across the Grand Canyon in May."

"That sounds nice. You have good potential."

"Thanks. I really enjoy it. I just never realized how much. And ever since I've been doing gymnastics, I've been too tired to hike. I realized that I like hiking better than gymnastics, even if it isn't as glamorous."

"Glamour is not a good reason to become involved in a sport. Desire is a good reason to get involved. And it sounds like you have the desire to hike."

Tess breathed easier now that the hard part was over. "I'm learning to ride horses, too," she continued, voice rising with excitement as she realized she would have time to ride now. Tess stood up to leave.

"Just a minute." Stefani scrawled a name on a notepad. "This is the name of the track coach at Chaparral Middle School. I assume that's where you'll be next year?"

"Yes." Tess reached out and took the paper.

"Since you like hiking so much, you just might like track, too. Tell him I sent you."

"Thanks," Tess said. She grabbed her backpack and headed out of the gym. She had done it! She let out a long breath.

As she approached the bench where Erin was reading, Erin dog-eared her page and put away her book. "Did you pay?"

"No. I didn't want to say anything until I saw how the coach reacted, but I told her I wasn't going to be on the gymnastics team."

"Really? Why?" Erin's backpack slipped out of her hand and onto the ground.

"Well, it was going to take too much time. I want to ride horses with you and hike with my dad and hang out. And I couldn't do all that stuff if I was in gymnastics. Plus, I was a little afraid my dad would make me quit church if I had too many activities."

"Oh. I'm sorry. Was the coach mad?"

"Steamed," Tess said. "I'm sorry, too, that I'm quitting. I could have been really good, you know."

"I know, Tess. But you are really good just as you are. At hiking, at watching kids, at being a friend. I wanted to tell you all that stuff the other day when you were talking about everyone balancing out, but Ms. M. interrupted us."

"Thanks," Tess said. "My mom told me not to compare myself to others. Now that I've stopped doing that so much, I do the things I like doing."

Erin nodded her agreement. "I know what you mean. When did you make your decision to quit the team?"

"While I was reading my love list from church yesterday. I was sitting under our grapefruit tree, reading what everyone said about me, and I felt better about who I really am. I realize I do have gifts. But it's nice to hear it from you all the same!" She smiled at her Secret Sister before continuing. "I prayed about what to do, and I felt really sure I should not be in gymnastics."

"It's great when you feel like God gives you a strong answer, isn't it?" Erin grew quiet. "Since you brought up the love lists though, I wanted to talk with you about something."

"Sure, what is it?"

"Well, can we talk about it in private?" Erin pulled her backpack over her shoulder as she saw Tess's mother's car approach.

"Sure. How about over our snack at the mall?"

"Okay. Do you still want to go shopping?" Erin asked. "I mean, I thought we were going to the mall so you could buy leotards, but you don't need them anymore."

"Well, we can look for your jeans and also spend the coupons. Plus, remember my surprise."

"What is it?" Erin asked eagerly.

"You'll have to wait to see. But you'll never, ever guess."

eighteen

Very Daring

Monday Afternoon, January 27

"Would you guys wait here for a second while I run around the corner?" Tess asked her mother and Erin as they sat down in the snack area.

"Actually, I have to phone my mom. Why don't we meet back here in a few minutes?" Erin said.

"Sure," Tess's mom said. "I'll wait till you two come back. Then I'll leave you guys to shop for an hour." Tess nodded, then quickly moved down the mall's corridor and out of sight. Less than five minutes later, she was back.

Erin wasn't though. Maybe the line was busy. Tess and her mother waited together.

"How do you feel about quitting the squad, Tess?" her mother asked. She burped a little. "This baby gives me indigestion."

"All right. Stefani won't give the fifty dollars back though." Tess held her breath while she looked at her mother.

"Hmm. Not good." Her mother hiccuped a little, then took a drink of her lemonade.

"Did you tell Grandma and Grandpa last night when they called? I mean, about my quitting?" Tess asked.

"No. Why?"

"Well, I know how much they think of Jane. I know they'll be disappointed in me."

"Oh, Tess. They might not be." Her mother didn't sound convincing.

"What about you and Dad?" Tess didn't look up from her drink, just chewed on the end of her straw and avoided her mother's gaze.

"What do you mean?"

"I know you're disappointed. I mean, I'm not a musical genius like Tyler or a snuggly baby like the one we're going to have. I know you were looking forward to seeing me do really great things in gymnastics."

"Is that what you thought?" Her mother clasped Tess's hand in her own. "I can see why you might. We haven't been very good about showing you how much we love and value you lately." She smiled. "It's not because we don't. I think you're a fantastic daughter, my firstborn! No one could ever replace you. And I know Dad was secretly glad you didn't join the team so you would have more time together."

"He was?" Tess raised her head, meeting her mother's eyes. "I thought he would be really upset."

"No. Although I'm sure he won't like the fifty-dollar business." Her mother smiled. "You're perfect just the way you are. Just the way your love list from church said. I think that church is pretty neat if they teach things like that."

"Thanks, Mom. I feel so much better."

Erin strolled over. "Ready to go?"

"Yes. Can you meet us here in forty-five minutes?" Tess asked her mom.

"Yes. Why?"

"You'll see. Thanks, Mom." Before her mother walked away from their table, Tess planted a kiss on her cheek.

"Should we get our ice cream?" Erin asked.

"Yes, of course you would remember the food!" Tess teased her. They walked to Cone Heads and ordered two cones, buying one and getting one free with Tess's birthday coupon.

"I'll have bubble gum," Erin ordered.

"Chocolate-chip mint for me," Tess added.

"What did you want to say about the love lists?" Tess asked, licking a little drip from the funnel-shaped cone.

"I feel sort of dumb," Erin said. "I wasn't trying to snoop or anything, but I read what you wrote to Melissa on her love list yesterday. I was just getting ideas of what to write. Anyway, I felt sort of bad, maybe jealous, that you guys were getting to be really good friends." She rushed on, "I mean, you've been busy the last week, and you hadn't even told me about baby-sitting for Mrs. Fye, and I just wondered, well, if I am still your best friend."

"Of course you are! You are the most important friend to me. More than that," Tess said, as she smiled into Erin's eyes, "you are my Secret Sister! But I can see how you might have felt bad. I forgot to call you a couple of times this week since I've been so busy with gymnastics. But now that I know what I really want to do," she licked her cone again, "we'll have more time together. To ride, or whatever."

"I'm so glad!" Erin said. "And I feel much better after telling you."

"Do you want to go to the bookstore? We have just enough time to spend that coupon before we meet my mom."

"Why did you ask her to come back in forty-five minutes?" Erin asked.

"You'll see." Tess giggled.

"Oh yeah, your surprise!" Erin smiled back.

After looking around in the bookstore for a couple of minutes, they each chose a book and headed toward the registers.

"Look. Charms." Erin pointed to a jewelry display case. Spinning it around, she looked for one for Tess and herself.

"Do you have enough money to buy one today?" Tess asked. "I do. We haven't bought one since Christmas."

"Yes, I think so." Erin dug into her wallet. "I do. Which one should we buy?"

"I don't know." Tess looked through the clear plastic display. She spied a Bible charm. "How about a Bible?"

"Sure," Erin agreed. They motioned to the clerk, who took two charms out of the case and rang them up with the girls' books.

"Secret Sisters forever?" Tess asked, fastening the charm onto her bracelet.

"Of course," Erin said, fastening hers on. They switched bracelets, like they always did to seal a deal.

"We'd better run, or we'll be late," Tess said, and they took off down the hall.

A few minutes later they met Mrs. Thomas. "Here I am. Where do we go now?" she asked.

"Right around the corner," Tess said. They walked in. It was a hair salon.

"Right this way, ladies." A natty stylist with a sharp-edged hairdo showed them to the back of the room. Tess took one look at the stylist's hair and almost changed her mind.

"Are you sure this is what you want?" her mother asked.

"Yes, I'm sure," Tess answered.

"So this is your surprise!" Erin said. "I think you'll look great with short hair. You're brave to do it, with all your fears and everything," She and Tess's mother stood right behind Tess as the stylist first washed Tess's hair then cranked the chair up high.

"This is what I want it to look like." Tess pointed to a picture from one of the girls' magazines she and Erin swapped.

"Okay." The stylist opened the mouth of her scissors and with a loud slice cut a long shank off Tess's hair.

"Don't look down," Erin whispered. The scissors flashed as they snipped, and about thirty minutes later the stylist roughed some gel into Tess's hair before blow-drying it. After five minutes of styling, she turned the chair around, and Tess stared at herself in the mirror.

Her mother and Erin stood behind her. No one said anything for a couple of seconds, and Tess started to worry. She didn't have to wait much longer though.

"I love it," said her mother, running her fingers through Tess's hair. "So grown up! Don't you feel lighter, freer?"

"Yes," Tess answered, breathing out. "You know, I love it, too."

"Cool and pretty," Erin agreed. "Even better than it looks on Michelle."

The stylist exhaled in relief and smiled as she spritzed another coat of hair spray on Tess's head.

Tess looked at herself in the mirror, caressing her shorter hairdo. She tucked a piece behind her ear. "I think so, too," she agreed, shaking her head and watching the strands tumble freely, shining under the stylist's lights. It seemed so easy she wondered why she had waited so long to do it. Turning to the left and then to the right, she rotated in her chair so she could see the new 'do from all angles. Smiling, she tipped her head toward her lap so the stylist could sweep stray hairs from the back of her neck with a big, soft brush. As the brush swished by, Tess felt the pleasant sensation of cool air rushing across her bare neck.

Why had she waited so long to try this? Once she believed the truth, she dared—even double dared—to be herself. Head still down, she glanced at her new Bible charm and remembered Psalm 139, the verses she had written down for her mother. God really had made her in an amazing and wonderful way.

Have More Fun!!

Visit the official website at:
www.secretsisters.com

There are lots of activities, exciting contests, and a chance for YOU to tell me what you'd like to see in future Secret Sisters books! AND—be the first to know when the next Secret Sisters book will be at your bookstore by signing up for the instant e-mail update list.

You can also find out how to order extra charms. See you there today!

Have Your Own Glow-in-the-Dark Party!

Your local bowling alley might have glow bowling, but if they don't, you can still have your own glow-in-the-dark party. Here's what you'll need:

1. A black light bulb (you can buy them at a home supply store, or even some supermarkets). Ask your parents to replace the light bulb in your room. After the party, they can switch it back.
2. White T-shirts
3. White or neon shoelaces
4. Glow-in-the-dark accessories. Some fun ones are necklaces, bracelets, glasses, and earrings. You can order party-sized boxes of these from the Oriental Trading Company at: 1-800-228-0475.
5. Other glow-in-the-dark stuff your local party store might sell

After you've set up and dressed up, play Yahtzee with glow-in-the-dark dice, which you can buy at many craft stores. Or purchase inexpensive black canvas sneakers, and write on them with glow-in-the-dark puffy paint, which can also be purchased at craft stores.

Have fun!

Art sure is fun, but fighting ain't.
Read these clues, then read "War Paint"!

Across

2 A battle or struggle
4 Enamel
7 Use a sponge, some water, and this to wash a car.
9 A large, expensive piano
10 What Tess does to earn money
11 All-out battle
12 Opposite of meanness
13 What Big Al and Tyler save for their contest; lint between toes
16 Birthday blow-ups

Down

1 Break the rules
3 Itza lotza fun to eat
5 Love your _____ as you love yourself.
6 Big problems
8 The popular crowd at Tess and Erin's school
13 Princess's crown
14 Romans 12:10 says to show this toward others.
15 Cast a ballot

Available May 1999:

#7 *Holiday Hero:* This could be the best Spring Break ever—or the worst. Tess's brother, Tyler, is saved from disaster, but can the sisters rescue themselves from even bigger problems?

#8 *Petal Power:* Ms. Martinez is the most beautiful bride in the world, and the sisters are there to help her get married. When trouble strikes her honeymoon plans, Tess and Erin must find a way to help save them.

The Secret Sister Handbook: 101 Cool Ideas for You and Your Best Friend! It's fun to read about Tess and Erin and just as fun to do things with your own Secret Sister! This book is jam-packed with great things for you to do together all year long.